PULP ADVENTURES™

BOLD VENTURE

Issue #46
Fall 2024

I0630305

CONTENTS

Rich Harvey | Publisher
Audrey Parente | Editor

Thanks: Philip Harbottle, Bart Pierce,
James Reasoner, Will Murray

Front cover: *Kong's Last Stand*
Back cover: *Santa Stihl*

***The following stories appear via
Cosmos Literary Agency:***

"Foolproof" copyright © 1946 by John
Russell Fearn, copyright © 2002 by Philip
Harbottle. First appeared in *Vengeance
Shorts # 2*, published by Gerald G. Swan

"Leave of Absence" © 1974 by John
Burke, copyright 2024 by the Estate of
John Burke. First appeared in *The Tenth
Ghost Book* edited by Rosemary Timperley,
published by Barrie and Jenkins Ltd..

A Thing Possessed copyright © 1971 by
Shelley Smith, copyright © 2024 by the
Estate of Shelley Smith. First appeared
in *The Seventh Ghost Book* edited by
Rosemary Timperley, published by Barrie
and Jenkins Ltd.

Editorial
AUDREY PARENTE

Yes, Zorro is happening for television

Bold Venture Press has been cranking out Zorro material for nearly a decade. BVP has the good fortune of holding publishing licenses from Zorro Productions, Inc. As a result, Bold Venture became the first (and *only*) publisher to reprint the orogonal Zorro stories by Johnston McCulley.

This connection has opened the door for opportunities. For instance …

Back on December 14, 2021, *Variety* announced Wilmer Valderrama made a deal to develop, produce, and act in a new "live-action Zorro series for Disney Branded Television."

On March 6, 2023, *Variety* also announced "*Game of Thrones*' Alum Bryan Cogman" would "serve as writer, showrunner, and executive producer" on the new Zorro series.

Wilmer Valderrama's book tour brought him to Miami, where Audrey Parente met the author.

A writers' strike broke the pace. Time passed with no further news about the Zorro plans. But Valderrama, who started his career as "Fez," the foreign exchange student in the sitcom *That '70s Show* (1998–2006), and currently plays Nicholas "Nick" Torres, an *NCIS* Special Agent on CBS, wasn't idle.

He's been active in several philanthropic

agencies, became co-founder of Harness (a group dedicated to connecting communities through conversation to inspire action), serves on the board of Voto Latino, and sits on the National Hispanic Media Coalition's (NHMC) Visionary Alliance (which aims to foster opportunities for Latinx talent in the entertainment industry through the Series Scriptwriters program and the Latinx Stream Showcase). Wilmer is also deeply involved with the military community, serving as a USO Global Ambassador, and participating in various shows worldwide.

He also became an author, and his book *An American Story: Everyone's Invited* is wildly successful. He made a book tour which included a stop near his birthplace in Miami, which gave Bold Venture's editor Audrey Parente the opportunity to meet him and present him with an array of Bold Venture books in English and Spanish.

Audrey took the opportunity to ask about the status of his Disney deal. On September 17, 2024, with his Press Agent and Book Publisher's representative

Audrey Parente met with Wilmer Valderrama, future 'Don Diego de la Vega,' and star of *NCIS* on CBS-TV.

standing nearby, his words were: "I can't give you any specifics, but Zorro *is* happening!" ∎

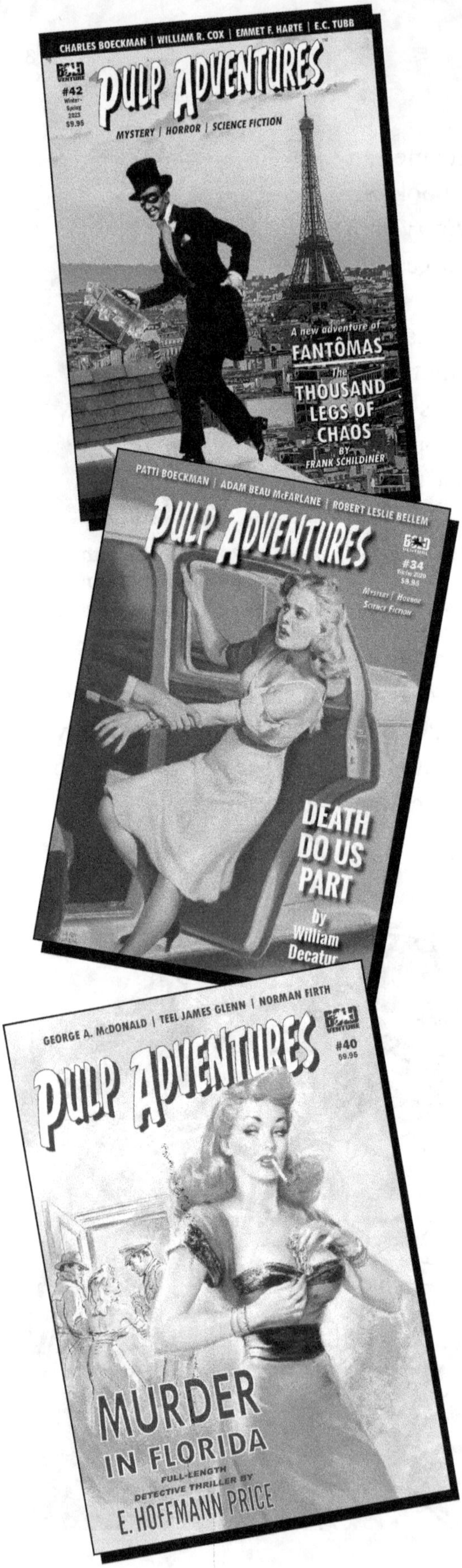

KING KONG

AND THE

WRONG WOMAN

by BART PIERCE

> "Why, there are dozens of girls in this town tonight that are in more danger than they'd ever see with me.
>
> — *Carl Denham*

KING KONG

PART ONE: STALKING HIS LAST VICTIM

By BART PIERCE

King Kong peers through the window at the innocently sleeping young woman. His giant invading paw thrusts through the open window probing toward the unheard silent screams of the terrified girl before pulling her upended into the windswept night, His supporting fingers loosen to allow the helpless victim's headlong plunge to her meaningless death on the cold pavement below.

She would quickly be forgotten as the spot-lights swing away from her insignificant life to follow the more impressive spectacle of her powerful man-like simian killer climbing higher and away from the emasculated chaos of the faint and frightened disarray of humanity below.

If you have seen the

This production drawing by Byron Crabbe, based on an original sketch by Willis O'Brien, imagines the "wrong woman" scene before even a script existed.

original 1933 version of *King Kong* in the last 50 years, you have likely seen the young woman, an unnamed actress, who sleeps in her high-rise hotel bed while the mighty Kong searches for his lost prize, Ann Darrow (a.k.a. actress Fay Wray).

Who was *King Kong*'s "wrong woman?"

The scene was crafted to haunt your memory, and almost 90 years after the scene was created, it still evokes an unnerving horror in its audience. And yet for many years, both the "wrong woman" and the actress who played her suffered the same fate, forgotten and dropped into obscurity.

Not a real surprise the actress is not remembered. Her namelessness was always intended. She wasn't a star, after all, just a "bit player" in an uncredited part. It was just a moment's work; just a chance to practice her acting craft and, of course, more importantly, to see a paycheck. After all, this was the height of the depression, and it was a long fall from grace if you could not pay the rent or afford a meal. How appropriate she should be playing an anonymous woman, pulled momentarily into the klieg lights, only to be callously cast off to a horrifically insignificant end. Perhaps it was an allegory the uncredited actress understood and could infuse into the tragedy of her role. Misfortune by the devil's own luck was certainly an allegory of the times.

King Kong, the greatest fantasy adventure of all time, had been woven in Hollywood, the city of illusions, by master dream weavers. Hollywood was a place where every nook and cranny, person, place, or thing, was subject to a flourish of the imagination, by the stroke of a magical pen or the intrusive eye of the camera's deception. The coming of sound to film had transformed Hollywood, subjugating it to the brawling economic powerhouses of a young country deep in its own titanic economic struggles to survive and define itself in a world driven by new and burgeoning technologies. And, in consequence, at the exact moment in time of the movie's release, Kong *was* king. The biggest and brightest star in the kingdom of Hollywood; he, and anything near him blazed in the transfiguring starlight of that image-altering machine, including the "wrong woman."

These were not the best of times for actresses in Hollywood. Women had attained the right to vote, but only a decade earlier. The bra had only recently become a popular garment, but never yet burned. The culture had not yet heard from the "#Me too" movement, but young women of *King Kong*'s time still understood survival in Hollywood — a minefield for the hopeful actress. The temperament of the times was clearly elucidated in the script by Kong's screenwriter, Ruth Rose, a former actress herself.

Dialogue with the three principal male leads in the early scene reflects the milieu as they discuss the special circumstances of taking a lone actress on a dangerous sea voyage. From KONG, Screenplay by Ruth Rose. Excerpts from the shooting script, dated September 6, 1932:

ENGELHORN
But it's different taking a girl into danger.
DENHAM
Oh, I suppose there's no danger in New York? Why, there are dozens of girls in this town tonight that are in more danger than they'd ever see with me.
DRISCOLL
(dryly) Sure. But they know <u>that</u> kind of danger.

Perhaps this would be

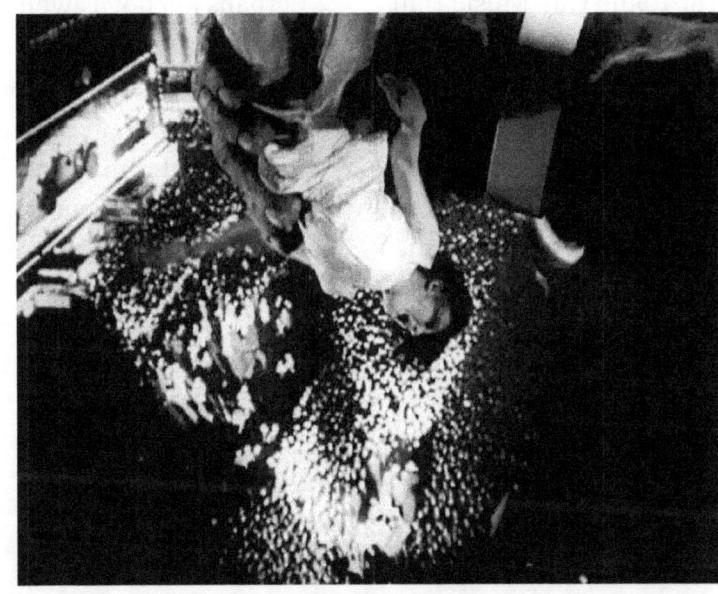

A vertigo inducing vista, projected on a translucent screen, is the backdrop for stunt double, Aline Goodwin, taking the fall from a full-scale hand of Kong.

the big break, not only for the girl Denham was trying to find for his voyage but also for the actress seeking to portray *King Kong*'s "wrong woman." Someone could see her uncredited performance, which might lead to more work. Maybe she might even have a shot at a credited role with more money and more work. Maybe!.. But that was not how this story was going to play out.

On March 2, 1933, *King Kong* was a hit! More than a hit, it was a phenomenon. This was the first movie big enough to premiere simultaneously at the two largest theaters in New York City, The Radio City Music Hall and the Roxy. Despite the 1929 stock market crash which had terminated the materialistic roaring '20s and initiated the Great Depression, and despite the new President Roosevelt closing the banks on opening night, despite everything, the movie packed both houses for weeks.

"Tremendous!" "Fantastic!" screamed the hyperbole of RKO's promotions department, and the critics agreed. No one had ever seen anything like it. And in the very middle of one of the greatest adventure films of all time, the uncredited, unknown actress sparkled in a moment of sheer horror as the anonymous victim.

There would be no extra money for our uncredited actress. There were no such things as residual checks to actors in 1933. But there was "opportunity." A great opportunity for an unknown actress to be elevated above obscurity, to be noticed and recognized. Being in a big hit meant the chance to become part of the dream, a thriving member of the "dream machine" that was Hollywood.

Perhaps it's not as well recognized now, in the current media-saturated world, but in 1933, movies were a unique magical experience, and Hollywood was the dream factory … the maker of myths. Hollywood had captured the populace's imagination. Film had grown and been nurtured from the peep show of its infancy to an industry of immense personal and sociological influence. Before Instagram and TikTok, Hollywood got its clicks and likes from audi-ence response cards, box office receipts, and letters from fans in fan magazines. The audiences chose the stars and Hollywood's star system protected, nurtured, polished, and refined the chosen for the presentation, titillation, and satiation of their theatergoers' fascinations. The false sense of intimacy they delivered was rabidly embraced by fans.

Anyone who has ever been seduced into losing a block of precious time by the enticing images on Instagram or TikTok can appreciate the addictive drawing power of these unsanctioned, informal images. The same voyeuristic-like kick and addictive quality provided by passive sharing of these credibly, informal and intimate images transformed Hollywood actors into a source of worship. They became stars.

Stars were the key, the enticement to the play in the magic mirror where Hollywood's dream weavers unfolded their chimerical tales for the price of admission. Stars were portals Hollywood sought and groomed to seduce the audience into "willing suspension of disbelief," the requirement to indulge in their meticulously crafted dreamscapes. Stars transported us to "Alice's view through the looking glass" and were, perhaps, Hollywood's greatest illusion. Worshiped as gods, and yet little more than chattel property, they were slaves to restricting and stifling personal contracts to the studios. Despite all their youth, beauty, and wealth, they were the studio's property to be bought, sold, traded, and controlled.

Yet 90 million people a week went to the movies because Hollywood had discovered these magic portals called "stars" could transport you into and through an otherwise unattainable and almost unimaginable experience in absolute safety. Armored in the pretense of a star and without fear of social repercussions, it was possible to anonymously indulge in the most intimate nuances of human character as they unfolded before your unaverted and unnoticed critical gaze.

No experience like this had ever existed before.

Wondrous and addictive voyeurism at its finest prevailed. Better than a fly on the wall, you could share the most clandestine secrets and emotions, lovingly etched in the features of huge self-subscribed, godlike visages across 30-foot screens, while being concealed safely in the dark. The experience was intoxicating and the source of the Hollywood motion picture's power.

This kind of power can appear threatening to some and the addition of sound to the movies only intensified the experience. The intensity renewed concerns about the need for censorship to "safeguard" the public from the tantalizing and insidious effects on this out-of-control cultural force ... the motion picture industry. The decision in the 1915 Supreme Court case of Mutual vs. Ohio had declared motion pictures were a business, pure and simple, conducted for profit, and not an art form nor a medium deserving free speech. As such, movies could be regulated by the states like any other manufactured product. Consequently, censorship

battles began early in the history of film and intensified with the coming of sound, the "talkies." Though some comity had been attained between the studios and the censorious church forces, that had spawned the original Hays Office Production Code in 1930, it was not to last. In addition to the censorship boards of different and overlapping state and local municipalities, the studios knew and accepted individual local exhibitors might snip out portions of the film they felt their local patrons might find offensive. Even progressive New York was affected.

During the Golden Age of Hollywood, there were no large film print orders (800-plus prints) for major releases like *King Kong*. The costly simultaneous release of a film countrywide would not become standard practice until the late 1970s when coincidentally, Dino DeLaurentis' *King Kong* was launched in 1976, helping to popularize this new style of distribution. Instead, one hundred or so prints were made and then "bicycled" across the country. When one theater was done with a print, it would be shipped to another theater in a different county, district, or state to be used there.

Prints tended to acquire more editing as they moved across the country because, in addition to the state and local censors, each theater would also make its own cuts in keeping with the moral attitudes of their particular neighborhoods. Consequently, theatergoers saw less and less of "possibly" offensive sex and violence as the print circulated (although discrete reels of a print could be replaced by the studio due to excessive wear or damage).

This affected the "wrong woman," because more often than not, she was excised, for violence, from the prints of *King Kong*. The results of these practices saw the "wrong woman" slip further into obscurity.

There was one possible saving grace for the "wrong woman." The studios discovered they could still make money from older films by re-releasing them and because of the tremendous success of *King Kong*, it could see many re-releases to theaters (and later to television).

But, alas, such was not to be the case for the "wrong woman." A national movement of Catholic conservatives felt the family, the foundation of society, was under attack from the outside by the subversive images being surreptitiously implanted in their films by the materialistic Hollywood studios. A Christian movement led by the country's Catholic minority wanted the interloper chastened and brought to heel. Hunger and desperation, inflamed by the economic depression, had intensified an

already entrenched family dynamic of "toxic secrets." Physical and psychological abuse, wantonness, infidelity, incest, cruelty, homosexuality, and homophobia, bigotry, misogyny, alcoholism, drug use, racism, antisemitism, and denial were considered family problems by the church. These vices should be dealt with by the family and within the family. And, of course, the church saw the family as the purview of the church, not mulch for the voyeuristic exploitation of a salaciousness-seeking Hollywood. Hollywood was the scapegoat but, more likely, the cause of the problem was closer to home. More succinctly, it was inside the home.

The church's solution was denial and censorship: push the genie back in the bottle. If the people didn't hear or see the secrets, they didn't exist. "Lead us not

KING KONG——*MARCH*, 1933
    REEL 8.—Eliminate all views of monster holding girl as he tears clothing from her body.
    REEL 9.—Eliminate all views of monster with natives in his mouth as he tears them apart.
    Eliminate all views of monster crushing natives with foot.
    REEL 10.—Eliminate all views of monster biting man whom he holds in his mouth.

New York censors demanded cuts to the perceived "strip scene" and Kong's violence.

into temptation." Hollywood was vulnerable, and well-organized boycotts of theaters orchestrated by Catholic leaders proved financially crippling. The studios caved. On July 15, 1934, Joseph Breen's Production Code Administration (PCA) effectively came to power.

From that point on, the Hollywood dream machine would heel to the conservative Christian's vision of America. The seductive power of Hollywood over its audience had been usurped for the purposes of Catholic minority leaders. The revised and strengthened 1934 production code had real teeth and the greatest retaliatory corrective reaction came in the form of a, sometimes less than subtle, conservative Christian misogyny putting the brakes on any freedom of expression for women. Especially sexual freedom. The materialistic "flappers" and the progressive movement of the roaring 20s were a target. The temptations of the biblical Eve were banished and all women on the silver screen, by the command of the newly reinvigorated pro-

Film frame at the head of all Hollywood studio films announcing the film had been cleared for viewing by the Production Code.

duction code, could only be truly fulfilled by becoming wives and mothers or, though still questionable, saints. Women seeking an alternate lifestyle or meaning outside of romantic love and family were portrayed as either lost, misguided, embittered, or just evil.

This solution had only shifted the blame and it would be 30 years before the traumatic dynamics of the era's American family could be publicly portrayed, let alone addressed, by the Hollywood film and the culture. Perhaps not coincidentally, this was the same time the teeth of the Production Code came to an end with the 1952

Supreme Court decision of Joseph Burstyn, Inc. v. Wilson, popularly known as the Miracle Decision. The Court overturned its previous decision and recognized that a film was an artistic medium entitled to protection under the First Amendment. This decision choked the production code to death by the early 1960s as the Hollywood motion picture ended up exploiting and inspiring a cultural cry for understanding by capitalizing on the dramatic portrayal of the impact of the conflicts, weaknesses, and threats of the dysfunctional American family.

Nonetheless, in 1934 the strict new production code was in force and

To an amazed civilization is exhibited a cowed brute whose origin can only be guessed at and whose story has even the news reporters thrilled. Ann, golden and glittering in a beautiful Paris gown, reluctantly agrees to Denham's wish that

Yes, "King Kong" knows fear, but it is for Ann. When photographers shove Ann about for pictures the Beast thinks his Beauty is in danger. Thunder rumbles from his throat. Chrome steel chains snap.

Driscoll rushes Ann into the hotel just across the street and into a room on an upper floor. "King Kong" gets out of the theatre by breaking out a wall. He saw Ann disappear into the hotel and now he climbs up its walls as easily as a fly. He

Ann now knows that nowhere will she be safe so long as "King Kong" lives. He has found her. He carries her to the roof of the building, but when Denham and Driscoll pursue him there, he returns

Promotional newspaper comic strips came closest to the film's presentation: "He (Kong) snatches one girl from her bed. Finding she is not Ann, he drops her, shrieking to the crowded street."

henceforth, all new films or re-released films would have to be reviewed and approved by the PCA. Some films were banned outright. Others, like *King Kong*, were shown mercy. These films could be shown, but only with the required cuts. But, unlike the local censors, these cuts were not only to prints but to original camera negatives.

The original source of the sin was consigned to the fires of the righteous Christian crusaders. Our now wronged "wrong woman" had fallen heir to nonexistence, never to be seen again. Her secrets would be buried forever.

Still, a tenuous thread of pre- and post-release

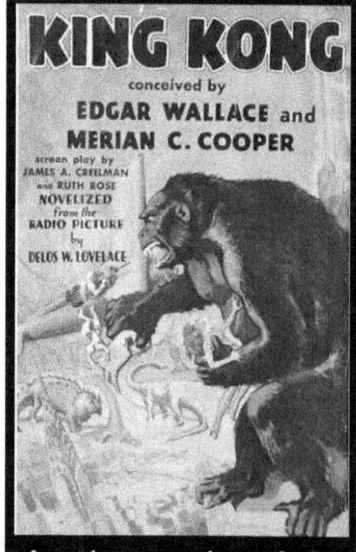

***Mystery Magazine* serialized King Kong in the February/ March 1933 issues: "He (Kong) reached the girl's window just as she was leaning out to see what was directly below. His big paw went around her. He gave her one glance and flung her back into the room, a look of disappointment and disgust on his face."**

A unique version of the "wrong woman," grabbed when making a date on the phone, was novelized by Delos W. Lovelace.

promotional material kept alive her story, if not her portrayal, of the "wrong woman" during the initial release of *King Kong* in 1933. A *King Kong* novelization came out before the movie as well as a contemporaneously released cartoon strip, and an abbreviated story summary released in two consecutive issues of 1933's *Mystery* magazine.

The Making of King Kong hardcover edition (left, 1975) and paperback edition (1976). Published by Ballantine Books.

Each of these had varying representations of the "wrong woman" sequence. The version that came closest to representing the deadly horror in the theatrical release was in the promotional comic strip released to local newspapers.

But ultimately, the thread was lost. Our vulnerable and doomed "wrong woman" actress would not surafce again until until March of 1964. *Famous Monsters of Filmland* magazine reprinted a modified version of the 1933 *Mystery* magazine serialization containing the same, nonviolent version of the lost victim, in which she is simply thrown back into her room by a disappointed Kong. Then nothing for five years until 1969 when Janus Films restored *King Kong's* missing scenes for a limited theatrical release. Janus unearthed a 16mm film collector who had the missing sections. They blew them up to 35mm and inserted them into a 35mm print for the limited release.

Soon afterward, the original 35mm pieces were found and inserted into the print, further improving the image quality. It turned out the 35mm nitrate film sections that had been clipped, per the censors' instructions in the '30s, had been kept by one projectionist. The "wrong woman's" performance had been restored. (NOTE: The 2005 release of Peter Jackson's *King Kong* coincided with a new classic *King Kong* release on home video. Generated from uncensored, nearly pristine preprint film materials, including the "wrong woman" sequence, Warner Bros. unveiled a further enhanced and restored version of Kong.)

But who was she? Another seven years went by before the release of the second edition of the definitive book, *The Making of King Kong*, a slightly revised, softcover version, copyright 1976. (The very successful initial release of the hardcover of *The Making of King Kong* was in 1975).

The newly revised text announced: not only did they have to shoot the sequence twice (once using the full-sized Kong head and finally using

Left: Sandra Shaw as "the woman who screams from the hotel window" in the original *King Kong* premier and teaser trailer. Right: RKO Pictures publicity photo of Sandra Shaw in 1933.

Sandra Shaw as the Countess in the comedy short, *The Gay Nighties* (1933). Her non-speaking part in this comedy short was the most screen time she ever achieved in a very abbreviated Hollywood career.

an enlarged image of the miniature Kong model projected in the window), but according to Kong's fans, the actress portraying the "hotel victim" had been in the film all along, even in the edited prints. She was "the woman who screams from the hotel window." She was played by a stunningly beautiful actress named, Sandra Shaw who, a year after her performance, would give up acting and marry top box office star, Gary Cooper.

Not a bad ending for an uncredited young actress. Not only was she recognized and restored to the silver screen, but she had escaped the difficult path and pitfalls of a struggling actress and found a life of wealth, comfort, and motherhood married to Gary Cooper, the prince of Hollywood. Couldn't get much better. Sandra Shaw had given up the possibility of a career and embraced the fulfillment of romantic love, beauty, and marriage. Surprisingly, the very image of Hollywood womanhood as coerced to be portrayed by the Christian censors, had proven true for the "wrong woman." A true Hollywood story: Sandra got the Hollywood fairytale ending.

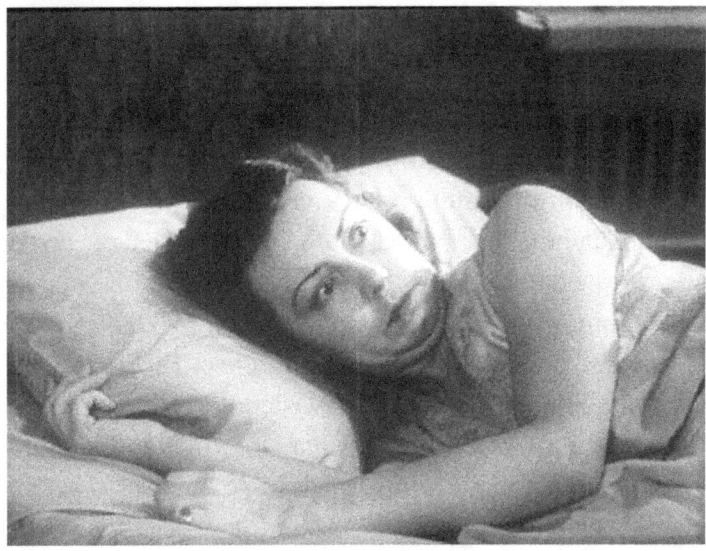

Rude awakening: Gertrude Sutton (above) in *King Kong*, and one of her publicity photos (below).

But the story isn't over. Jump to 43 years later, on January 23, 2019, someone on the Classic Horror Film Board noticed "the woman who screams from the hotel window" and the "hotel victim" (A.K.A. the "wrong woman") don't look like each other at all. "The woman who screams from the hotel window," definitely, looks like Sandra Shaw, a striking, raven-haired beauty. But the "hotel victim" (A.K.A. the "wrong woman") … Not so much.

In a follow-up on January 29th the face of *King Kong*'s "wrong woman" was found to belong to a little-known "bit player" named Gertrude Sutton, not Sandra Shaw.

Gertrude Sutton had been rediscovered and recognized for her performance. She was born on September 1, 1903, in Butte, Montana, died May 17, 1980 (age 76) in Los Angeles, California. She had been married twice and had no children. She also had 52 credits as an actress from 1929 to 1944. She mostly played in small, uncredited parts, often portraying the lightly comical, slow witted or confused service person as she did in a minor speaking role as a maid in the *King Kong* sequel, *Son of Kong* (1933). This, too, is a Hollywood story. Not nearly so grand as the myth-making Cinderella story represented by Sandra Shaw and her marriage to a prince of Hollywood, but it certainly echoes a closer tone to the ring of truth.

But what would lead the authors of *The Making of King Kong* to name an obscure, unbilled, unnamed actress like Sandra Shaw as the "wrong woman," when the actual performer was Gertrude Sutton?

The co-author of *The Making of King Kong*, Orville Goldner had worked on the film *King Kong* and his co-author, George Turner, said Goldner read and approved everything. The authors also had access to extensive materials and resources provided by the many surviving principal personalities who created *King Kong*, including access to the surviving producers, directors, credited screenwriters, lead actors, and other behind-the-scenes personnel. Surely one of these principals must have known the truth. As quoted in his book, *All the Kings Men,* George's son, Douglas Turner wrote: "the interview material in this publication (referring to *The Making of King Kong*) is not a single interview, but rather it is culled from multiple conversations — both person-to-person and over the phone — .as well as a long-running correspondence and notes in the margins of rough manuscript drafts of *The Making of King Kong* that occurred over the course of several years from 1969 to 1976."

Michael H. Price, who assisted the authors of *The Making of King Kong* said they had a 16mm print before 1969 (these restored prints had been available to collectors since the early '60s) with all the formerly excised scenes restored (including the "wrong woman" sequence). Price said the film was watched many times during the writing of the book and it appears the difference between the two actresses went unnoticed. Then, what or who would cause the authors to extract and apply the name of Sandra Shaw to the "wrong woman" in their definitive book on the making of *King Kong*? … Especially when the revised version would have allowed them time and opportunity to recheck and correct any possible mistakes in the initial release? What did they miss?

Well, to quote Yoda, the sage-like master of *Star Wars*: "There is another."

And so, yes, there is another story.

It should've been a movie: an epic battle, a quest, by the heroic forces of imagination against the crippling god-like power of a brutal economic reality in an era of cataclysmic transformation. It could only happen in Hollywood. The most extraordinary talents and personalities of the times; adventurers and magicians, poets, dreamers, and schemers coalesced around and clashed in the capital of illusion to defiantly spawn the most improbable fantasy and greatest illusion ever presented on the silver screen. In denial of the tumultuous earth-shattering change surrounding them… they had succeeded.

So, we will need to return to the turbulent days of the Golden Age of Hollywood to find our answers. All levels of the film industry were struggling for survival amid condemnation, conflict and uncertainty. The coming of sound had left carrion husks of former stars rotting on the wind. Our "wrong woman" was but a leaf upon a momentarily serendipitous breeze.

The forces that drove and battered her existed beyond her scrutiny. So, her story can only be witnessed through the reflected struggle of the extraordinary personalities being buffeted by the seemingly overwhelming forces surrounding them. These were the larger forces that held sway in her life. Without their dreams and fears, innovations, surprises and regrets, mingled with the spicy metallic tang of desperation, we cannot tell her story. But, by tasting the flavor of the times through the characters who savored them we can draw our conclusions and, perhaps, discover some suspects.

In 1932, the soft censorship of the original, ineffective Hays Office Production Code was in force. The strict production code, under Breen, had not yet been instituted and the studios had become adept at working with, and around the censor's rules, a time now referred to as the "pre-code era." Good roles, portraying strong financially, emotionally, and sexually independent women, were making careers for actresses like Barbara Stanwyck and Joan Crawford. The studios were pushing the boundaries of good taste, sex, nudity, and violence. But it would be the image and memory of the face and persona of Fay Wray that would draw Kong to the "wrong woman's" high-rise window and Fay Wray's Hollywood film persona had been built on her playing the "good girl" in her previous studio contracts. Fay's costar, Bob

The sensually explicit *Tarzan and his Mate* (1934) presaged the stricter censorship of the Breen code administration and also "borrowed" the spectacular elephant stampede from *Chang* (1925) the Cooper/Schoedsack "natural drama."

Armstrong, in reminiscing about another "sweet and lovely" actress from his silent film days recalled, "She was almost as nice as Fay — but of course, *nobody* is that *nice*." But in 1932, at the start of Kong's production, she was a free-lance artist, and no studio was contractually or financially vested in her image. In other words, she was not a studio property who needed to be protected or nurtured for future use.

She had felt pressured from Kong's earliest scenes to show more flesh. Her close friend and confidant, the alluring star, Dolores del Rio, had helped presage this Hollywood call for the "flesh of stars" during her abbreviated RKO contract when she starred in *Bird of Paradise* (1932) just before *King Kong's* production. This pre-code Hollywood feature saw Dolores del Rio playing an island princess who is sacrificed to a prim-

itive God. (This sacrificial theme inspired Merian C. Cooper's storyline for *King Kong*). In a highly publicized scene, she seduces Joel McCrea during a nude swim sequence. (Note: producer, Merian C. Cooper slipped by the censors' scissors with a swimming scene for one of the more titillating moments of *King Kong*. As Fay came out of the water after her perilous fall from Kong's cliffside retreat … the censors failed

This early pre-production drawing — made prior to Fay becoming the beautiful blonde object of Kong's unwanted affections — was prepared by Kong animator, Willis O'Brien. Used as promotional material, it suggested a more explicit portrayal of Fay's strip scene.

to catch her exposed breast.

Del Rio's nude swim inspired a similar and more explicit scene with Maureen O'Sullivan (being doubled by Olympic swimmer, Josephine McKim) swimming naked with Johnny Weissmuller in *Tarzan and his Mate* (1934). The tasteful, though flagrant, nudity outraged the censors and provided adequate ammunition for them to secure the severe crackdown of the production code, instituting the removal of Kong's "wrong woman" scene for its re-release in 1938. But Fay resisted the constant cajoling to show more flesh for a scene where Kong, comfortably seated in the safety of his mountaintop retreat, examined, and played with his diminutive prize by sniffing, prodding, and, like pulling petals off a flower, pulled pieces of clothing off her body.

Kong EFX technician and animator, Orville Goldner wrote: "He (Cooper) wanted her to do the strip scene in the nude, but she wouldn't do it. If it weren't for her refusing to do it, we'd have had the girl running around naked. Between Cooper (a.k.a. producer, Merian C.) and Obie (a.k.a. effects wizard, Willis O'Brien), they did their best to get her clothes off."

But, Goldner added, "She had a maid who watched over her." (Note: Hazel Fortado became Fay Wray's stand-in and companion during *King Kong* and continued in this role through many pictures. She married *Kong*'s assistant director Walter Daniels in 1934.)

Fay's reticence to shed her clothing emerged because of a charming naivete and fragility she exuded even into adulthood. A likely contributing factor was an unpleasant, early family dynamic of an enforced sexual innocence backed up by traumatic shaming from an intimidatingly willful mother.

Fay had been harshly schooled in the contradictory and confusing politics of Hollywood flesh several years before. Shortly after marrying Academy Award-winning writer, John Monk Saunders (considered by many, the handsomest man in Hollywood), Motion Picture Magazine (August 1928) published a partially nude photo of an artfully draped, 14-year-old Fay taken by photo artist, William Mortensen. Fay's mother had assigned her daughter's guardianship to Mortensen who ferried her to Hollywood. He was later to become a successful studio photographer and Fay always credited him with bringing her out of her shell and giving her a sense of self-worth as well as procuring her first acting job in Hollywood.

Before Kong became the "dark lover" of her life, there was her husband, John Monk Saunders. Upon learning of the magazine photograph, Fay's abusive, flagrantly unfaithful, and controlling alcoholic husband ... backed up by the power of her harsh and religiously eccentric mother ... brutally shamed the 20-year-old Fay. He warned she could lose her career and her studio contract with Paramount Pictures if they found out. Fay knew the protection and comfort of a contract (i.e., a regular weekly paycheck) was important in Hollywood. A girl's gotta

Fay Wray with her new husband, Academy Award winning writer John Monk Saunders and (below), starring with her frequent early costar Gary Cooper in *Legion of the Condemned* (1928).

eat. The paycheck was also important to her mother and her husband. (In 1936 amid a sagging career, and custody battle, the mentally disturbed, Saunders twice kidnapped their newborn daughter, Susan, and went into hiding. The traumatic incidents were resolved, but within a year of their 1939 divorce, Saunders was dead by his own hand.)

During the shooting of *King Kong* Fay was no longer contracted to Paramount. She was primarily a freelance actor for the rest of her life, with no studio having a financial interest in maintaining her previously well-tended image. So, in the land of the dark lover, she had learned to protect herself.

The creator/producer of *King Kong* was Merian C. Cooper. He had discovered Fay Wray's Ann Darrow and his "wrong woman" reflected in the eyes of a bewildered and uncomprehending anthropomorphic force of nature, *King Kong*. Kong was a beast that had seized his imagination and launched him on a holy crusade to realize his vision, "I wanted to produce something that I could view with pride and say 'There is the ultimate in adventure.'"

Cooper was a larger-than-life character. An explorer and adventurer akin to the fictional, Indiana Jones. He was a romantic who was inspired and aspired to the honor and heroism of his heroes. His favorite book was *The Four Feathers* (which he read in 1919 while a prisoner of war in a Russian prison camp). It is the story of a man, branded a coward by his friends and seeking redemption by performing heroic acts to save their lives.

Cooper was an individualist and adventurer who thrived on placing himself in the middle of the action and a "Southern gentleman" testing himself against the toughest the world could offer in pursuit of honor. He leaped into the middle of the worst battles (of World War I, II, and more) for what he considered "the good fight" with less concern for his own well-being and great concern for those he helped and fought with. (During WWI, surrendering to the inevitable, he escaped onto

Producers, Merian Cooper and Enest Schoedsack (above) on a huge mobile structure they built to film massive action scenes in *The Four Feathers* (1929). Fay Wray's performance (below) showed Cooper she embodied both an adventure seeking innocence and a delicate feminine sexuality that made her the perfect Ann Darrow for *King Kong*.

the wing of his doomed plane for relief from the unbearable pain of the flames consuming himself and the cockpit.

Realizing his gunner and friend, though gravely injured, was still alive, He climbed back and landed the plane with his elbows and knees, saving himself and his friend. The German pilot who shot them down was so impressed by Cooper's extraordinary skill and bravery battling impossible odds that he landed his plane in the field and escorted them to the German doctors to demand they be cared for. He probably saved their lives. Cooper would carry the disfiguring burn scars on his hands and arms for the rest of his life.

During World War II, he would divest himself of his airline stock so he could not be accused of profiting from the war. He was "a man of his word" (a rare thing in all times) and a soldier of fortune who sought the company of other like-minded individuals.

After the Great War, he formed a partnership with just such a man, camera-man Ernest Schoedsack, to make documentary films in the unexplored wilderness. Schoedsack's gruff Midwestern exterior concealed a heart of gold and the sensitivity of a true artist. Their slogan was "distant, difficult, and dangerous."

The financial and dramatic success of these films brought the attention of Hollywood. Cooper found he could be equally at home in the tropical jungles of Siam (A.K.A. Thailand) and the high finance concrete canyons of New York. He was an internationally recognized personality whose Southern military heritage granted him entrance to financial halls of power the immigrant heads of Hollywood studios could never dream of in the rampantly antisemitic business climate of the day.

One of his business hustles helped place David O. Selznick at the head of RKO Studios. Selznick repaid that debt by supporting Cooper's dream project of a giant gorilla battling primordial creatures and modern civilization.

Only a few years earlier, Cooper's aspirations of exploration and adventure were quashed as he saw the world growing smaller and more civilized. Cooper was a passionate promoter of early air power with a childhood fascination for gorillas and exploration. These frustrated romantic dreams of adventure ignited a vision of a giant primordial ape battling for his existence against attacking airplanes from the peak of the highest skyscraper in the modern world. This vision would possess him and drive him to the heights of Hollywood, the dream-shaping capital of the world.

At 39 years old, Cooper was short, stocky, and balding with a direct, showman-like manner. Fiercely intelligent, with a photographic memory he was a dynamo of activity and he could be overpowering. Friend, fellow adventurer, and spy, Marguerite Harrison described him perfectly: "eyes light blue China buttons, a pugnacious jaw and an aggressive manner. He was disdainful of all the refinements in life which were 'soft' in his opinion …. Stubborn as a mule, moody, quick-tempered but generous, and loyal to the point of fanaticism.... Merian's turn of mind was essentially dramatic. He was forever striving for startling climaxes and sharp contrasts." His biographer and friend, Rudy Behlmer wrote: "Merian C Cooper was quite a guy. Difficult in many ways — yes. Very difficult at times. But quite a guy."

His exuberant personal style could come across as over-the-top and inflated self-aggrandizement because the actual truth he spoke of his life and experiences was so extraordinary. He was a man of exceptional physical courage and the truth of his life sounded like an exaggeration. He had a boyish enthusiasm and charm people were drawn to and an astounding record of success. In paying the high dues he felt he owed the world and his family honor; he had beaten the odds and far exceeded any expectations.

A confirmed bachelor, he represented many of the attitudes of his day: In her 1935 biography, *There's Always Tomorrow*, Marguerite Harrison,

bristled at Cooper's earlier sexist views about women. She described a 31-year-old Cooper as "a compound of southern chivalry and Oriental contempt." She went on to say, "He had inherited the idea that 'nice' women were made to be set on pedestals and worshiped. On the other hand, he was convinced that they were brainless creatures fit only to mind home and bear children." And yet, as the production of *King Kong* came to a close, Cooper would, ironically, mirror the fate of his giant anthropomorphic creation.

Kong would safeguard his beloved Ann Darrow to the precipitous heights of the Empire State Building only to experience a calamitous fall from its peak. Cooper too would be felled by the face of beauty when he succumbed to love and married his Ann Darrow, a rising young actress named, Dorothy Jordan (For love, she turned down the star-making Ginger Rogers role as Fred Astaire's dancing partner in the Cooper produced, *Flying Down to Rio*). Upon achieving the heights of power as head

of RKO studios, he would be felled from this pinnacle by a heart attack. Cooper prophesized his own destiny when he wrote an Arabian poem to open his movie:

> *And the prophet said:*
> *"And lo, the beast looked upon the face of beauty, And it stayed its hand from killing.*
> *And from that day, it was as one dead."*
> — *Old Arabian Proverb*

But Cooper would rise from the ashes.

By the end of 1931 Cooper had been hired by the new head of production at RKO, David O. Selznick, to help save the beleaguered studio from a rapidly approaching threat of bankruptcy. Selznick had chosen the right man. Cooper and his partner, Ernest "Monty" Schoedsack, had proven they could make better movies for less money when in 1925 they had disappeared, alone, into the most remote jungles of Siam (A.K.A. Thailand). With $70,000 and a passionate willingness to utilize anything and everything that the challenging and unforgiving environment could provide, they persevered with endless and unrelenting innovation to create a picture from whole cloth so sensational that, to quote Kong's Carl Denham, "… They'll have to invent some new adjectives when I come back." They returned with a thrilling and dramatic, "natural drama" that grossed 1.7 million dollars (it netted more than *King Kong*'s initial release).

Nominated for an Academy Award, *Chang's* climactic elephant stampede was so spectacular that it was stolen by MGM for the ending of their first two box office bonanzas that launched Johnny Weissmuller's career as Tarzan. *Chang* was Cooper's calling card for entrance to Hollywood.

Cooper was wholeheartedly on board to prove RKO could become an efficient, low-cost company that would produce high-quality motion pictures and *King Kong* was at the top of his list to prove his point.

In a seemingly serendipitous turn, one of the several films in production that Selznick assigned him to evaluate, upon his initial arrival at RKO, was a troubled and highly speculative jungle picture called *Creation*, about the fight for survival of a small group of people stranded in a lost world of dinosaurs.

Cooper found little worth in the story but realized that the film's impressive technical wizardry, propelled by the genius of Willis O'Brien (A.K.A. "Obie") and his crew, could provide him the answer to manifesting his vision of *Kong*.

Before the coming of the new year, Cooper had metamorphosed *Creation's* floundering $1.2 million production, into a positive proposal for a leaner, meaner, and grander production of *King Kong* at one-third the cost. Cooper believed that the same maverick spirit of innovation that had succeeded in an unforgiving and demanding Siamese jungle would prove itself supremely adaptable in the equally demanding wild jungles of Hollywood studio filmmaking.

Cooper was a force of nature. He had given his word to Selznick, and he intended to succeed. In fact, Cooper had refused to take a salary for the job until he had proven his worth. This was a work ethic he and Selznick shared. The young Selznick had done the same thing when he first went to work at Paramount and MGM.

David O. Selznick was one of Hollywood's wonder boys and the recently named, youthful head of RKO studios. Selznick inherited his unquenchable and purportedly reckless drive from his father, Lewis J Selznick, one of the early and more successful hustlers in the budding silent film industry. Unlike his father, who just enjoyed the financial game and hustle of the film industry, David loved making films and he was good at it. Filmmaking wasn't his career; it was his religion. He set himself on a course to prove he was the best film producer in the world. He could accept no less. Within eight years he would produce what is arguably the greatest motion picture of Hollywood's golden age: *Gone with the Wind* (1939).

He was a tall, bespectacled, average-looking 29-year-old armed with abundant energy, a keen mind, and more than his share of charm. He had recently married the daughter of MGM's Louis B Mayer, head of the greatest studio Hollywood ever produced, and was soon to be a father. In what played as the casual misogyny of the pre #MeToo era of the 1930s and keeping in tone with the movie studio heads of the times, Selznick indulged himself in numerous, and usually meaningless, 30-minute affairs with delivery girls, secretaries, actresses, and whatever attractive female was available.

Merian C. Cooper (left), and David O. Selznick (right) meet with financier, Jock Whitney.

When Selznick had become vice-president in charge of production at RKO Studios the previous year it was on the brink of bankruptcy. He had promised he could save them from disaster by making quality pictures for less than the other studios. He had begun a series of severe cost-cutting procedures, but he had a problem. Quality pictures meant stars because they were what drove the Hollywood picture machine. Stars were the studios' access to their audience. Stars told the stories that Hollywood sold. But stars were extremely expensive, and RKO had very few stars under contract. Selznick would have to either borrow them (i.e., pay a premium price to another studio for a loan-out of a valuable star), buy them (i.e., find high-price stars without existing contractual obligations and put them under expensive contracts) or create new stars (i.e., find untried personalities and develop them under inexpensive contracts) and all on a tight budget. Finding new stars would be the least expensive. But it was very

David O. Selznick

risky, a crapshoot really, because no one ever knew who the audience would be drawn to. The studios could not create stars. They could polish, present, and protect them, but the audience had to first discover and embrace them.

Selznick used all these methods but chose to lean heavily into finding and developing new stars. The most frequent technique embraced by Selznick to create new stars was what was known as a "term short-option agreement" or the "trial contract" (a.k.a. "the heartbreak contract").

These were short-term contracts of 3 to 6 months that paid prospective stars about $30 to $150 a week in 1932 (a decent wage in the Depression era). Although, in truth, the studios could fire them whenever they wanted to, they did contribute sporadic training in acting, costuming, makeup, and sometimes screen tests. To earn their salaries, the development of the nascent stars entailed them posing for publicity photos to be

The Camera Catches Them in Their Off-Moments

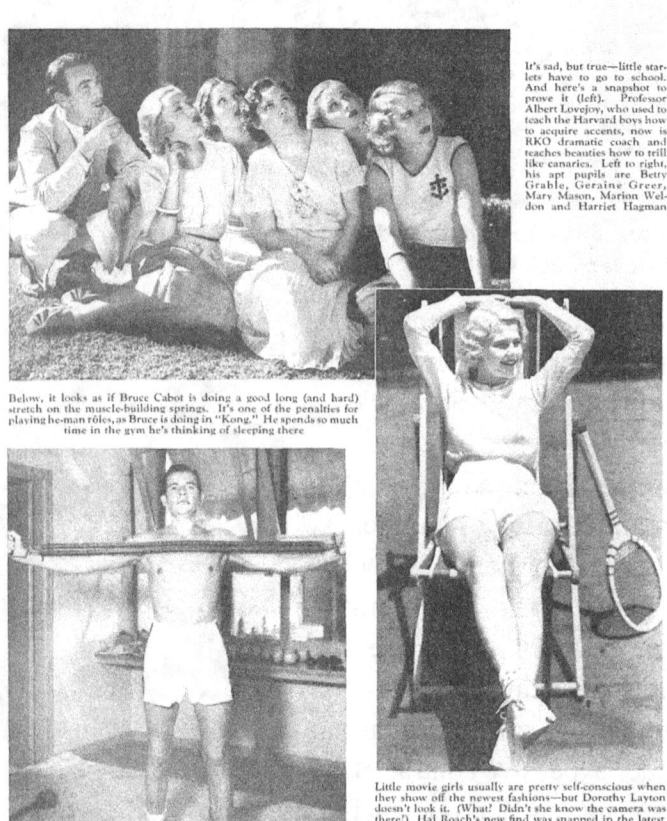

It's sad, but true—little starlets have to go to school. And here's a snapshot to prove it (left). Professor Albert Lovejoy, who used to teach the Harvard boys how to acquire accents, now is RKO dramatic coach and teaches beauties how to trill like canaries. Left to right, his apt pupils are Betty Grable, Geraine Greer, Mary Mason, Marion Weldon and Harriet Hagman

Below, it looks as if Bruce Cabot is doing a good long (and hard) stretch on the muscle-building springs. It's one of the penalties for playing he-man rôles, as Bruce is doing in "Kong." He spends so much time in the gym he's thinking of sleeping there

Little movie girls usually are pretty self-conscious when they show off the newest fashions—but Dorothy Layton doesn't look it. (What! Didn't she know the camera was there!) Hal Roach's new find was snapped in the latest garb for tennis—a fancy knit sweater, silk shorts and polka-dot socklets

Radio Grooms Tyros Unused to Big Dough For New Star Parts

Hollywod, June 20.

Radio is basing its future star list on a new crop of young femme players, being recruited from the stage and from purely amateur ranks. In few cases is the weekly tap more than $50.

Back of the idea is the same urge that prompted Warners to comb Broadway recently for young and cheaper stock. Studios are of the opinion they can halt the telephone number idea of salaries for players, now current, by bringing in at low pay youngsters who haven't been spoiled to exorbitant demands by previous contact with Hollywood.

Within last three weeks Radio has added six prospects who are getting good spots in pictures with an opportunity to show what they've got. As many more get similar chances within the next month.

In each case players are given long-term option contracts, which do not tie the companies up for more than three months if the candidates are sour, but allows studio to hold on for five and seven years if any of them prove hot.

Sextet now getting a chance to win their spurs are Dorothy Wilson, stenographer, recently here from Minneapolis; Phylis Fraser, amateur from Oklahoma; Julie Haydon, with northern California stock experience; Harriet Hagman, from small parts on Broadway; Mary Mason, from Pasadena Community Players, and Betty Furness, recruited from an eastern dramatic school

Fan and trade magazines promote Starlets: (left) *Motion Picture Magazine*, **Nov.1932. Camera catches up-and-coming starlets in their off moments. Betty Grable, Geraine Greer, Mary Mason, Marion Weldon and Harriet Hagman. Bottom of page is Bruce Cabot training for 'Kong.' Meanwhile,** *Variety* **for June 21,1932 (right) reports how RKO Radio Pictures grooms young starlets under cheap, "heartbreak contracts."**

Nine Radio Pictures starlets, all in a row. This is how they looked when Ernest Westmore lined them up to get their first "make-up" lesson. They are Dorothy Wilson, Phyllis Fraser, Rochelle Hudson, Peg Entwhistle, Harriet Hagman, Eleanor Pose, Julie Hayden, Betty Furness, and Sandra Shaw.

(Below) Maureen O'Sullivan and Jimmy Dunn often go to athletic events together. Jimmy is with Fox. Maureen is an M-G-M player.

Photo by Bachrach

Photo by Robert W. Coburn

RKO starlets Dorothy Wilson, Phyllis Fraser, Rochelle Hudson, Peg Entwhistle, Harriet Hagman, Eleanor Pose, Julie Hayden, Betty Furness, and Sandra Shaw get their first "makeup" lesson in *New Movie Magazine*, Nov. 1932. Delores del Rio (below) promotes *Bird of Paradise* (1932).

By
TERRENCE COSTELLO

Motion Picture presents the greatest show on earth— the intimate goings- on of the stars at work and play

One of the first lessons you learn when you break into the movies is to smile with your toofies showing. The five RKO starlets who have just won brand-new contracts, getting down to earth, show you how they do it. Left to right: Julie Haydon, Mary Mason, Harriet Hagman, Rochelle Hudson and Phyllis Fraser

***Motion Picture Magazine* promotion of five new RKO Pictures Starlets. (Left to right) Julie Haydon, Mary Mason, Harriet Hagman, Rochelle Hudson and Phyllis Fraser.**

Photoplay Magazine for March 1932

"We stay slim…or we lose our contracts" …say Bruce Cabot and Fay Wray

How to keep weight down and energy up .. that's the problem movie stars face.

Recent RKO short-term-contracted, Bruce Cabot, with his future co-star, Fay Wray. They promoted Borden's Malted Milk in *Photoplay Magazine,* March 1932, two months before they would work together on *King Kong*.

given to fan magazines … bathing suit photos were popular … and modeling for fashion photos, helping to entertain visiting theater-men and film distributors at Hollywood conventions, and showing up to enhance multiple kinds of promotions for movie houses, grocery stores, or dedication ceremonies, etc. And, of course, they had to appear in public to be photographed with other stars and starlets to polish their image as "personalities" of note. Sometimes there were product promotions for which the studio, not the contracted, received the remuneration.

The most desired assignments by these starlets were for "bit parts" or "walk-ons" in actual movies which presented them the opportunity of being recognized and appreciated, even, possibly, placed in the credits as a "featured player." These parts increased the possibility of larger roles, or the extension of their contracts, with more money, and the possibility of fame. A piece of the dream.

There were also less formal methods that a young actress could use to burnish her career possibilities. Invites to private parties and events beckoned, where directors, producers, writers, and other influential persons would attend. But a budding young actress had to "know the score" to be able to navigate this perilous path. If a struggling young starlet was escorted by a prestigious Hollywood personality, she would understand and expect the date, most likely, would

not end at the door. There was no #MeToo movement and scandal was carefully (as well as corruptly) and meticulously suppressed by the studios.

In his efforts to reduce RKO's bottom line, Selznick initiated a campaign, sending scouts throughout the country to locate new and less expensive "stars" to develop. He signed several "personalities" to short-term contracts in early 1932 (including Bruce Cabot who would appear as the hero in *King Kong*). Most were young women because Selznick was soon to film a popular book, *Thirteen Women*, requiring lots of young female talent (and women were

the movie's most reliable and avid fans).

This was an opportunity to introduce several prospective stars to a theater-going audience at a low cost. Perhaps one or two of them might even catch the fascination of the audience, making them exploitable and thus making it worthwhile to polish their stars by developing them further into the typecast personalities fans craved to see.

Selznick must be given the credit (even if it was to his own advantage) for showing a prolific interest in developing his starlets and giving them screen time. As a result, Selznick would introduce the wildcard into our cast of characters: Harriet Hagman, the other "wrong woman."

'King Kong and the Wrong Woman' continues on the next page.

KING KONG

PART TWO: THE OTHER WOMAN

Gertrude Sutton had portrayed the part of the wrong woman on the screen. But, before Gertrude, there was another, quite different, portrayal by Miss Harriet Hagman. The authors of *The Making of King Kong* had told their "wrong woman" story. They'd known that the sequence had been shot twice and with two different scripts. What they seemed not to know was that there were two different actresses for the sequence.

Three months before Gertrude performed before the cameras, Harriet Hagman had played a very different "wrong woman." Harriet was an actress even

more obscure and unknown than Gertrude or Sandra.

But who was Harriet Hagman? And what were the motivations and practices of the dominant characters that influenced the tides and pulled the strings that animated her?

Harriet Hagman was a 24-year-old, dirty blonde, Finnish beauty living in Brooklyn, New York. The purported, former Miss Norway (according to the hype) had been discovered by Broadway talent scouts and brought to New York as part of a sweep of European countries. She had gotten her first taste of Hollywood in January 1932 dancing in the chorus in Universal's racy pre-code crime drama *Night World* (a rematching of Mae Clark and Boris Karloff who had appeared the

Night World (1932) promotional poster (top) and photo (above) with Alice Adair, Consuelo Baker, Edna Callahan, Mae Clarke, Gloria Faythe, Bess Flowers, Harriet Hagman, Mary Halsey, Amo Ingraham, Bee Stephens, and Beatrice Hagen.

This stage door marquee welcomed Earl Carroll's bevy of beautiful showgirls to work.

previous year in Universal's Horror masterpiece, *Frankenstein*).

But Harriet was "discovered" by RKO, in New York, while performing in *"The Earl Carroll's Vanities of 1930 Broadway Revival,"* which starred Jack Benny. *Earl Carroll's Vanities* was a hugely successful revue which capitalized on a bevy of scantily clad, lovely young women providing décor for some of the top comedians of the day. The show had been plagued with scandals from the beginning. In 1929, one wild after-hours party, which also involved a famous "naked girl in a bathtub of gin" incident, was splashed across the newspapers.

In Harriet's own 1930s show, nine cast members were arrested for "indecent performance." Earl Carroll's tagline: "Through these portals pass the most beautiful girls in the world" was emblazoned on the front of the theater, and Harriet was but one of a bevy of beautiful young women who decorated the stage for the headline talent. She was, however, the only one who managed to secure a highly prized Hollywood contract.

She succeeded in winning a ticket to Hollywood and a contract, but she had

Harriet Hagman, in 1931 promotional photo, is described as "Jazz Age flapper and theatre showgirl in decadent, lavish costume designed by Charles LeMaire and Vincente Minnelli for Earl Carroll's Vanities."

> Those arrested are Irene Ahlberg, 19, who won the title "Miss America" this year; Constance Trevor, 22; Eileen Wenzell, 20, known as "Miss St. Louis;" Frances Joyce, 19, "Miss San Francisco;" Kay Carroll, 22; Naomi Ray, 22; Jimmie Savo, comedian, 31; Betty Veronica, 18, and Faith Bacon, 20.

Clip of newspaper article on arrests for *Earl Carroll's Vanities 1930* indecent performance.

a problem. She had previously, under assumed names, secretly married her boyfriend, West Point cadet and football hero, Henry Sebastian. Hollywood studios didn't like young starlets with husbands, so she had to convince him that her moving 3,000 miles away to the Hollywood Babylon was a good idea.

Henry was not in a good position to argue. Their secret marriage was not allowed under Naval rules. This was a court-martial offense were he caught in a violation of the 95th Article of War forbidding a West Pointer to have "a horse, a dog, a mustache, or a wife."

While his paltry pay from the military couldn't support them both, Harriet was already earning several times a cadet's stipend. Her salary would be increased to $100 a week under her new RKO contract (a healthy income in an economy where many families lived on $18 a week or less). This was at the height of the Depression and "a girl had to eat." Of course, a shot at fame, fortune, and a career were also alluring. It took a while.

Claiming illness, Harriet arrived a couple of months late, on April 4th, to begin her three-month

RKO contract … Henry had caved.

Harriet was, from the first, typecast as a "flapper type." A product of the economic boom years following World War I, known as the "Roaring Twenties," "flappers" were materialistic, stylish young party girls who smoked in public, drank alcohol, danced in jazz clubs, practiced sexual freedom, and, in general, challenged traditional notions and norms about femininity and the role of women.

She did "bit parts" and "walk-ons" as "flapper types" in several films, often with some other hopeful young starlets of the day, including Betty Grable, Betty Furness, and Phyllis Fraser. Harriet, as a seasoned showgirl, apparently "knew the game and the score." She was ambitious, determined, and capable. She knew how to survive and navigate a system in which you were often either predator or prey, and she wanted to be a star. Arriving in Hollywood, she immediately got a "featured role" as one of the *Thirteen Women* in the movie of the same name. Quickly after she

"Flappers" rejected customary feminine roles, threatening the bedrock of the American family's societal norms.

Left: Silent film icon Louise Brooks in *Pandora's Box*. Right: Silent film star Joan Crawford, with Dorothy Sebastian, and Anita Page in *Our Dancing Daughters*, which promoted the 1920s "flapper" image and launched Crawford to stardom.

got a small speaking role as a manicurist in a scene with the lead male, Ricardo Cortez, in *Is My Face Red?* Unfortunately, you do not see her face in the Cortez scene, and *Thirteen Women* was not successful (initially released in July 1932, it was pulled from release and radically re-edited and shortened for a planned re-release in September).

Despite these disappointments, Harriet must've been feeling pretty good about this time. And she had reason to be optimistic and excited. On July 1st, her contract was extended another three months, and she was lined up to do several more "bits" in several different films. But the most exciting was *Kong*. She was to have a "solo speaking bit" in the biggest film on the lot. As part of his plan to develop new stars, Selznick was using this "bit part" to push his starlet. A glamour shoot, a photographic session with the head of the department, portraying her as a seductress in the negligée she would wear in *King Kong* would be used to promote her. She would be announced in the trades and, it appeared, she would be a "featured player." Things were looking up for Harriet. Her star was rising, and she was being pulled into the spotlight. The Hollywood dream beckoned.

Harriet had no way of knowing her hopes and dreams were about to be dashed to the ground. She was, like her successor, Gertrude, about to be cast into obscurity by the Hollywood machine.

Kong was a unique and promising opportunity for Harriet. But months earlier, the executives in New York were less enamored of this unusual film and its financial promise. Cooper's attitude that, "...there was nothing a man could mentally conceive that

Silent film "It Girl" Clara Bow epitomized the 1920s "flapper."

the cameraman could not recreate or exceed…" was revolutionary and before they would approve the full production of this unique and risky film, they would first authorize a minuscule $10,000 budget for a short "test film." The test amounted to some of the most spectacular animated scenes with Kong that would be included in the finished film. They had been pitched by Cooper and pushed by Selznick, to demonstrate how the speculative and unproven, new special trick effects for the picture were viable and affordable.

Above and below: Publicity glamour shots of Harriet in her "Kong" nightgown, prepared by RKO head photographer, Ernest Bachrach.

But, before long, an open secret emerged in Hollywood: Selznick had been surreptitiously redirecting resources from other pictures to this production, referred to by some as *"Cooper's Folly."* Though these actions were well-intentioned, they could frequently extend over the line of officially prescribed authority.

A good example of these irregularities is found in a cost-cutting idea Cooper had developed before coming to RKO. He thought by cross-pollinat-

ing two films they could share resources. The idea was good. To keep the budget of the "test film" for *King Kong* in line, he and Selznick initiated another jungle feature, *The Most Dangerous Game*, which required an elaborate modular jungle and cliff-set be built. Very conveniently these sets provided Cooper with exactly what he needed for his test film. They appeared to be designed more for *King Kong* than for *The Most Dangerous Game*.

So, while his friend and co-director on *King Kong*, "Monty" Schoedsack, directed the jungle scenes for *The Most Dangerous Game*, Cooper, using the same sets, managed to synchronously shoot not only his authorized test footage, but also, almost all of the live-action jungle scenes for the yet-to-be-authorized, full production of *Kong*. Cooper never stopped pushing forward. He had no intention of failing. He continued to film the unauthorized

footage and build his production up to and throughout New York's evaluation of the "test film." (Note: *The Most Dangerous Game* proved to be both a good and successful film on its own). Selznick admitted years later: "… one of the biggest gambles I took at RKO was to squeeze money out of other budgets of other pictures for this venture." He didn't so much believe in Kong … he believed in Cooper.

The presentation of the "test film," made for a

15 Players Are Being Groomed for Stardom by RKC

RKO IS GROOMING 15 FOR STELLAR HONORS

Film Daily July 11, 1932, announces Harriet Hagman, Bruce Cabot, and others being groomed for stardom.

(Continued from Page 1)

parts in completed or coming productions. They are:

Phyllis Fraser and Mary Mason, who will be cast in pictures to be put in work next month; Harriet Hagman, Julie Hayden and Jill Esmond, who will be seen in "Thirteen Women." Creighton Chaney, who has an important part in "Roar of the Dragon," starring Richard Dix, and in the RKO Van Beuren serial, "The Last Frontier." Gwili Andre, who has just finished work in the Dix picture and will have a more important part in "Mysteries of the French Police"; Katherine Hepburn, "Bill of Divorcement"; Arlene Judge, "Age of Consent"; Rochelle Hudson, "Liberty Road"; Anita Louise, "Phantom of Crestwood"; Dorothy Wilson, "Age of Consent"; Betty Furness, "Liberty Road"; Bruce Cabot, "Kong," and Eric Linden, "Age of Consent."

Parts Being Assigned to Stellar Candidates in Individual Films

Fifteen young players are being groomed by RKO for stardom in a like number of Radio Pictures features for the 1932-33 schedule. All but two of the embryo stars have already been assigned important

(Continued on Page 3)

"claimed" $10,000 (rumor has it, Cooper contributed $5000 from his own pocket), had hit it out of the park when presented to the New York execs. At the end of July 1932, *Kong's* budget was approved for $400,000, but the increasingly nervous New York office would demand more and more assurances the *Kong* situation was under control. Neither Selznick nor Cooper wanted any more heat or eyes on their project which might spook the men who held the keys to the money, and their ambitions as production #601 went into full gear.

Selznick, like all film moguls, was a high-stakes gambler. He was nearing the end of his one-year contract with RKO and preparing to negotiate a new one. If successful, the new contract would include a substantial bonus, which he needed to address his extravagant lifestyle and out-of-control gambling debts a consequence of high-stakes card games played with other Hollywood moguls and principles.

But there were dangers on the horizon. Even before

Another promotional photo from the RKO studio photographer's camera would capture Harriet's image as the same seductive "flapper" she had successfully played on the New York stage of *Earl Carroll's Vanities*.

Kong's test was approved, he knew Cooper would soon have to ask for a significant budget increase. Still, Selznick saw putting Harriet in the "wrong woman" role as a good bet. An easy, low-cost, speculative wager for launching an appealing image he thought he could sell to both the public and New York.

Promoting Harriet's image as a sexy and fresh new face, placed in peril, in the middle of RKO's high budget, high-profile film, would increase New York's stake in Kong's success. And if the public embraced her as a budding new star it would be another win he might add to the plus column in his contract negotiations with New York.

Harriet's photographer, Ernest Bacharach, head of RKO's still department wrote: "If the player is a newcomer to the studio and especially if he (or she) is new to pictures, I must take great care to have my portraits coincide with the personality that the studio — through casting, make up and costuming — hopes to build up for their new luminary. I must make my camera see the newcomer's personality as the public will discover it on the screen, many months hence."

understand.

On July 22nd, about the same time that New York ok'd the production of *Kong*, and nine days before Harriet was to go before *Kong*'s cameras, Ruth Rose, the wife of *Kong*'s co-director, Ernest Schoedsack, would turn in her very first screenplay ever, a treatment rewrite of *Kong* for which she received a budget-conscious $150 a week ($850 less than James Creelman, whom she replaced). The treatment included the newly expanded and restructured "wrong woman" scene. Now enhanced with dialogue, the new scene could not have been better for Harriet if it had been written for her … and most likely it was. Ruth Rose knew the challenges of the New York theatrical life. She had tread the boards of the stage herself and she knew writing to an actor's strengths was how Hollywood created stars … and Selznick needed stars.

But the new script had also included a budget bombshell not yet announced: a storyline involving a lavish set piece with a sacrificial ceremony

Both the microphone and the camera seemed to like Harriet and once again, she was being reliably cast as a "flapper." In her first "featured role," she'd played an attractive young showgirl who falls to her death. This makes her fall-to-her-death in *Kong*

a comically literal typecasting of her first role at RKO, but with an improved twist for Harriet. The part of the "wrong woman" played to her strengths: a beautiful and sexy young flapper, on her own, and on the hustle in New York. This was a role Harriet Hagman could performed by a huge cast of extras before a great wall. Cooper had found the "great wall set" on RKO's Pathe' lot months before. The structure had originally been built for the silent epic, *King of Kings*. An impressive ancient architectural piece, it had inspired and contributed to the scope of Cooper's new sacrificial offering storyline already inserted into an earlier mid-June draft of the script. So, just as Harriet began shooting her "wrong woman" sequence, Cooper would need to ask for an additional $117,000 to complete these and other augmented scenes. Despite an earlier warning from Selznick's New York nemesis, the NBC/RKO president Merlin Aylesworth, in the June 15th *Film Daily* stating: "The billion-dollar motion picture industry faces bankruptcy in 90 days unless drastic measures are introduced..." the New York office, ultimately said yes. They too desperately needed a hit.

But New York was nervous. RKO's parent company RCA was beginning to sense they may no longer be able to bail them out if money got tight. They too were now feeling the pinch of the sinking economy engendered by the worldwide economic depression. By November, Selznick would receive a copy of a memo confirming RCA could no longer guarantee the existing loans secured by all of RKO's material assets, nor could he expect financial support from their former electric affiliates, General Electric and Westinghouse, that were recent court-ordered divestitures. He was on his own.

```
KONG climbing building.

Another hotel room. A woman in negligee at telephone.

                    WOMAN

        Yes, Jimmy, it's Mabel....You bet I'm glad you're
        back...I got your postal....Talk louder, Jimmy,
        there's fire-engines going by. I can't hear...
        Sure I saved the evening....Nine o'clock'll be
        swell....And say, wait till you see my new outfit...
        It's a wow, kid...All right, I'll be there...Say,
        when did I ever break a date with you, honey...

KONG at window. He reaches in, picks her up, pulls her out

window.

Exterior, hotel wall. KONG looks at her, sees she isn't Ann,
```

Script excerpt of Ruth Rose's original July 22 "wrong woman" scene performed by Harriet Hagman.

Camera and production crew prepare to shoot Cooper's new budget-ballooning sacrificial ceremony before the massive, redressed set from 1927's epic on the life of Jesus, *King of Kings*.

Selznick would announce in December he was jumping ship to Hollywood's premiere studio, MGM, for an extremely lucrative production deal. While walking out of a February test screening in San Bernadino of, the still-under-production, Kong, he suggested Cooper excise the movie's beginning and open on the island. Cooper uncharacteristically snapped back at his friend and most unflagging supporter: "To hell with you, David. You go make those fancy pictures of yours at Metro, this is going to run!" It would seem Cooper, named to succeed Selznick as Head of Production, felt betrayed and abandoned in the midst of their unfinished struggle to complete Kong and prove they could make high-quality, economically efficient films.

The smell of desperation for what threatened to be the imminent approach of an RKO bankruptcy heightened a kind of "buyer's remorse" in New York that was expressed in increasingly tighter budget controls and more calls for austerity in spending across the board. Kong was still an unknown commodity. It had not yet seen the face of its audience. And it was risky. None of the actors were bonified stars who would rate above-the-title star billing on the film.

Kong was the headliner, the title character, and no one, including Walt Disney, had ever done a feature-length film with an animated character as the star and lead player. New York feared the budget might climb to as much as a million dollars like the recent Bird of Paradise had (Selznick had pulled the production from its Hawaii location back to the studio and created costumes props and sets that would be adapted for use on Kong). They were increasingly complaining about ballooning expenses they wanted addressed by Selznick and Cooper.

Kong's production was essentially an instinctual process patterned after the ad hoc filmmaking of the Cooper/Schoedsack "natural drama," *Chang*, which had been improvised from the available resources of the jungle. Kong was being conjured in the alchemy and syntax of the same adventurer's vision but with the surrounding wealth of possibilities offered by the wonderfully practical and creative ether of a Hollywood studio. A star would be birthed and made manifest with an inanimate puppet. While the script was in a constant state of flux, being written and rewritten on the set, Cooper, under duress, began stripping his production down to bantam weight. While countering the punches of the heavy hitters, he raced toward a threatened and unsure finish. Amid the mounting pressures, the indomitable Cooper could be found striding through his embattled production, beating his chest and defiantly declaring: *"I am King Kong!"*

On August 15th, Cooper sent a long memo to B. B. Kahane, the financial watchdog at the studio, attempting to calm New York's fears and hostility. He pointed out the awkward, lengthy, and lurching nature of the production was an expected learning curve resulting from creating a unique and spectacular production using new and innovative methods. He assured Kahane: "All my production heads and myself have … spent the last several weeks, going over each item of the script, and every trick shot in detail, and have eliminated everything, except what was absolutely necessary, and, as far as our combined opinion is concerned, have brought the picture cost down to bedrock for this script." But nothing would ease their fears. (Note: After Selznick's departure at the beginning of the year, and the hammer blow of RKO's bankruptcy and negotiated receivership, Cooper ascended to become RKO's production chief; "We literally had no money… Three times I was told to close down the studio by the board of directors in New York. And each time Maxie [Max Steiner, composer of the precedent setting score for *King Kong*] came to me and said, 'Coop! Merian! I'll work for nothing. Don't close her down.' And I never did."

On the first day initiating Kong's full production, the "wrong woman" shoot with Harriet, began awkwardly. It was the first shoot that would composite *Kong* in a New York scenario and they would shoot only the scenes inside the hotel apartment set. Studio records indicate the director, Schoedsack, expected

Unused rear screen plate, "photographic test" images of (left) Obie's earlier "long faced" Kong model and (right) a later version Kong model that would be used in the finished "wrong woman" scene. Cooper rejected this approach in favor of the "big head." (Note: The dark horizontal bar is likely a climbing support for the Kong model and would not be seen in the final composite.

the scene (and another scene of an interrupted poker game enacted on the same redecorated set over the same days of August 1st and 5th) would use a rear screen projection of the animated Kong model. The film of Kong would be projected onto a partially translucent screen placed outside the set's window to give the impression he was climbing up the building. A full-size prop hand would be used to smash through the window and pull Harriet from the room, the same method to be used in the finished scene of the movie. But that is

How the rear projection was intended to be filmed for Harriet's "wrong woman" shoot …

not what happened.

Cooper decided, instead, to use a recently completed, full-size head of Kong as an alternative to rear screen projection of an animated Kong. Cooper had promoted the construction and use of the "big head" for close-ups and extreme close-ups even though "Obie" and his modelmaker, Delgado, preferred the use of animated miniature puppets. Perhaps the prepared animation of Kong was unconvincing or there were other technical or scheduling problems. Or, perhaps, Cooper just wanted to justify the cost of an expensive prop he'd built during the production of the "test film," but barely (if ever) used.

Whatever the reasons, they settled on the trolley-mounted, full-scale mechanical Kong head to perform outside the window because, as Cooper later wrote in 1966: "My say was final in every department of the picture … In this particular picture I was the Creator and Boss."

Unfortunately, Cooper quickly developed a dissatisfaction with the film that came back from the "wrong woman" shoot. The expensive "big head" prop, which rolled around on a large platform on wheels and which he had insisted on, contrary to the wishes of his chief animation team, did not give a convincing impression Kong was hanging off the side of the building. This situation compounded Cooper's problems with New York's continuing, scrupulous reexamining of the budget. He was about to request a budget increase for the newly augmented scenes in the script. But, if he re-shot the "wrong woman" scene now, it might spook the bean counters. They might see the failure of the very first full production shots of Kong, after its recent approval, as a harbinger of future problems.

… and how the "big head" was finally used for Harriet's "wrong woman" shoot.

The "Son of Kong," reserviced and fully articulated hand, with Robert Armstrong.

Obie on RKO lot in front of the "big head" prop on a trolley.

Harriet's performance, with her wavy blond hair and flowing nightgown being pulled upright out of the window, looked exactly like the shot in the following scene when our blond heroine, Fay Wray, is pulled out the same window. This repetitiveness might lessen the distinctive quality and impact of Fay's peril, not to mention a "flapper" possibly overshadowing the beauty of his lead actress. Equally troubling, he'd had Ruth Rose give *Kong's* script a storybook, Victorian-like style with a chaste heroine he referred to as his "woo girl." As described by Cooper, she: "had to be innocent and

Harriet's performance had gone from becoming a possible feather in their cap to a choke chain around their neck, a haunting specter of out-of-control costs. And there were other things that would grate on him.

The "big head" prop in progressive stages of production.

How Harriet's scene *may have* appeared. The "big head" peers at Mabel on the phone convincing her prospective evening's meal ticket that she's interested in his proposition.

(Artwork by Drew Pierce 2024)

brave — I wanted her to be what I call 'a woo.' A beautiful young girl, who dresses in a very feminine way, puts bows in her hair, and looks up to a man, accompanying everything he says with 'woo, woo, woo.'"

He had found his "woo girl" in Fay Wray, and Cooper didn't really want the distraction of a beautiful flapper competing with his chosen heroine at the climax of his Victorian-styled romantic fantasy. Selznick's scene would distract the audience from the story of his handpicked beauty in his fairytale romance. To quote Kong's captor, Carl Denham, whose characterization both writer, Ruth Rose and actor, Robert Armstrong based on Cooper himself: "Well isn't there any romance or adventure in the world without having a flapper in it?"

Yet, four days later, the trades announced Hagman's addition to the "Kong" cast. But, even before Harriet could read of her "featured player" status in the September 6th *Variety*, Cooper would be ordering that animation of Kong looking through the hotel window be prepared for a rear screen projection shoot on September 2nd. Schoedsack would shoot a different, but very similarly composed, interior scene of Fay being recaptured by Kong on that same re-dressed, high-rise hotel set. This time it would be Fay, Bruce Cabot and one of his stunt doubles, King Matora, who would

16-year-old dancer (and Fay Wray double) Edith Haskins, sports newly added manacle when pulled from the hotel set on September 3rd. The positioning of her legs and dress indicate she's seated on an inside support so she can kick her legs as she is pulled out the window.

Hollywood Production
Week of Sept. 5

Studio Placements

RADIO
'Eighth Wonder'
(22nd week)
D—Merian C. Cooper
Ernest Schoedsack
A—Edgar Wallace
Merian C. Cooper
James Creelman
C—Eddie Linden
S—None
Fay Wray
Robert Armstrong
Harriet Hagman
Frank Reicher
Jim Flavin

Caryl Lincoln, Cecelia Parker, Frank Glendon, Francis Ford, 'Lost Special,' U.

Kurt Neumann, to direct 'Son of a Sea Cook,' U.

Ginger Rogers, 'You Said a Mouthful,' WB.

Harriet Hageman, Noble Johnson, Steve Clemente, 'Kong,' Radio.

Left: Sept. 6,1932 Variety announces Harriet Hagman in KONG with "featured players."
Right: August 9, 1932 Variety prints Harriet Hagman's studio placement with "featured players."

take the assault of that same, full-sized prop arm.

The "big head" was gone and replaced by the Kong animation projected on a rear screen. Also, in this new scene, the full-size arm smashing through the window sported, for the first time, *a new wrist manacle that Kong would not acquire until his escape scene to be shot later in the schedule*. When Cooper added the manacle he created, perhaps purposely, a continuity problem. This scene was intended to immediately follow the "wrong woman" scene.

But there had been no manacle in Harriet's scene. When they had shot Harriet's sequence a month earlier, no one had mentioned anything about the need for a wrist manacle to maintain continuity. Harriet's "wrong woman" scene would have to be re-shot with a manacle if they intended keeping it. Hearing about unnecessarily creating needed re-shoots would probably have upset New York. Hopefully, they didn't have to know.

Once the usage of rear screen projection proved satisfactory in this new scene, Cooper returned to his preferred, original concept of the "wrong woman." Harkening back to the earliest pre-production drawings, and the very first draft of Kong, he'd wanted a young and innocent girl ripped from her happy dreams to the horrifying reality of a giant anthropomorphic nightmare.

We don't know what Cooper thought of Harriet's performance, but clearly, he felt he no longer needed a scheming blonde flapper, and he would recast the part accordingly.

On finding actors, Cooper said, "We never tested anybody. Most of the time you'd see people in something, and you'd get a pretty good idea of what they could do…" He would "diplomatically" postpone the reshoots (though they would not be identified as reshoots) another two months hence.

Selznick would play his Harriet cards close to the vest. So, with Cooper's decision to scuttle Harriet's performance, Selznick would waste no time.

Relieved of any impetus to renew Harriet's contract option and safe from any New York blowback, he added Harriet's name to the budget cuts column of the studio spreadsheet to satiate New York's ever-increasing demands for austerity. A week after being published in *Variety* as a featured player in *Kong*, the same paper announced that RKO had decided not to pick up her option. Harriet would be unemployed by the end of the month.

Harriet's failure was not substantially her own fault. She was always dangling from someone else's thread, a pawn in someone else's game. Sadly, its utility for sacrifice is a pawn's greatest strength and this pawn would need to be sacrificed because of conflicting motives, mistakes, and miscalculations on the part of Selznick and Cooper who were under immense pressure, budgetary and otherwise.

She might've stayed. Other young women with similar opportunities had toughed it out and ultimately made it. Betty Grable worked under minimal contracts performing bit parts for years before she got the break making her a star.

September was tough for budding stars in Hollywood. The news was full of the shocking, shooting death of Paul Berne. He was recently married to the rising star, 21-year-old, platinum blonde, Jean Harlow and there was fear the scandal might ruin her career.

Closer to home was the tragic end of 24-year-old Peg Entwhistle. Twelve weeks before, as young starlets, Harriet and Peg had shared their first dialogue scenes together on the set of *Thirteen Women*. Peg was a truly gifted young actress who had been on a short list for the Katherine Hepburn, star making role in "*A Bill of Divorcement*." (Bette Davis in her autobiography cites Peg's portrayal of Hedvig in the 1925 stage production of Henrik Ibsen's *The Wild Duck* as her inspiration to become an actress).

RKO's financial woes had forced an abrupt termination of her contract. Within a week, the *Los Angeles Times* reported Peg had leapt to her death from the top of the Hollywood sign. If Harriet was the least bit superstitious, she could not help but feel haunted that Peg had died in a fall, the same way as Harriet's most prominent portrayals on the silver screen.

Though Hollywood

```
dw        298     EXT. HOTEL - NIGHT

                  FULL SHOT - Kong still climbing.  He stops at a window.


          299     INT. ROOM IN HOTEL - NIGHT                         102

                  MED. SHOT - Girl in bed.  The window is open.


          300     EXT. HOTEL - NIGHT

                  FULL SHOT - Kong appears.  He reaches in his hand,
                  pulls girl out of bed and through the window.


          301     EXT. HOTEL - NIGHT

                  MED. SHOT of the girl in Kong's hand.  He looks at
                  her and throws her away.


          302     EXT. HOTEL - NIGHT

                  FULL SHOT of girl falling from the 16th floor.
```

The original "wrong woman" scene from the first draft screenplay of *King Kong*, originally titled *The Beast*. It was written by Edgar Wallace, based on Cooper's notes. Though the script closely resembles the "wrong woman" scene in the finished film, it does not portray the "screaming woman" and the "wrong woman" as the same character as would later scripts. *(Courtesy of UCLA Library Special Collections Performing Arts)*

Promising actress, Peg Entwistle leapt from the "Hollywoodland" sign after her contract cancellation by RKO.

seemed less promising for a hopeful 25-year-old actress, Harriet stuck it out through October, just long enough to be called in for a bit part as one of the "Sandrich Company" in RKO's Oscar-winning Best Short Subject Comedy of 1934, *So This Is Harris*. (Director, Mark Sandrich would shortly find great success directing the Fred Astaire, Ginger Rogers musicals).

But Harriet had another very different contract she'd signed with a soldier who would probably not wait forever. She'd had her shot and she'd taken it. The dream was gone. Time to go home. Another true Hollywood story …

**'King Kong and the Wrong Woman'
continues on the following page.**

" He's always been king of his world, but we'll teach him fear.
— *Carl Denham*

KING KONG

PART THREE: THE INVESTIGATION: ILLUSIONS ABOUND

Little more than a week later, on November 9th and 16th, "bit player," Gertrude Sutton went before the cameras as the anonymous "wrong woman," for the first time. Schoedsack, as he had earlier with Harriet and Fay, shot only the apartment interior of the "wrong woman" scene.

Once again, they used a rear screen projection of the miniature animated Kong outside the window. Previously, Harriet and Fay's stand-in, Edith Haskins, had to brace themselves while seated inside a less technically sophisticated, large prop hand. But for safety and facility, Gertrude would

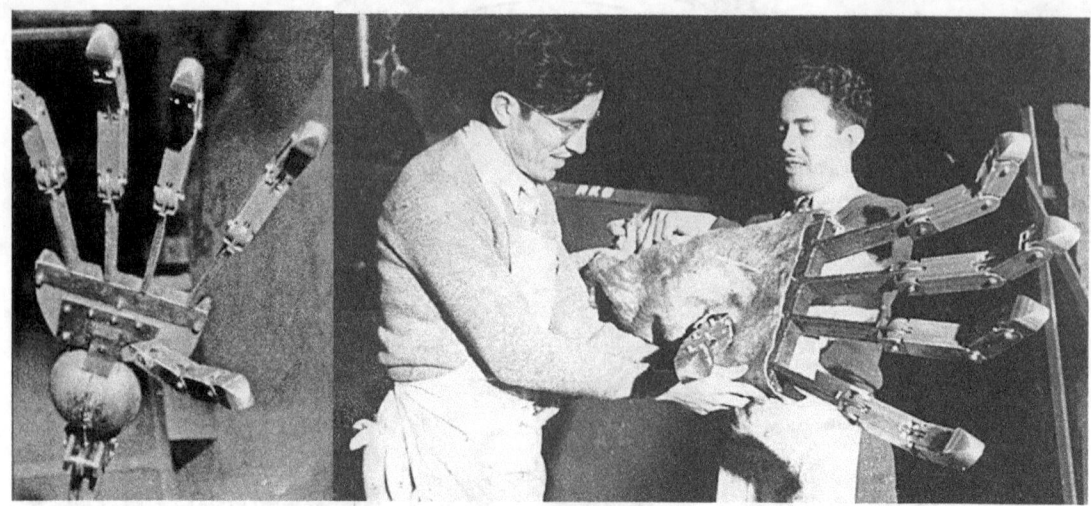

Victor and Marcel Delgado hold Kong's partially completed and improved prop hand. It now had the necessary thumb joint that correctly extended into the palm of the hand. This improvement allowed a firmer and more realistic grasp of the actor in the palm of the hand. It worked like a large stop motion armature. The stiff joints of the fingers and redesigned thumb could be manually manipulated to "cup" like a real hand and hold the actor safely in its palm.

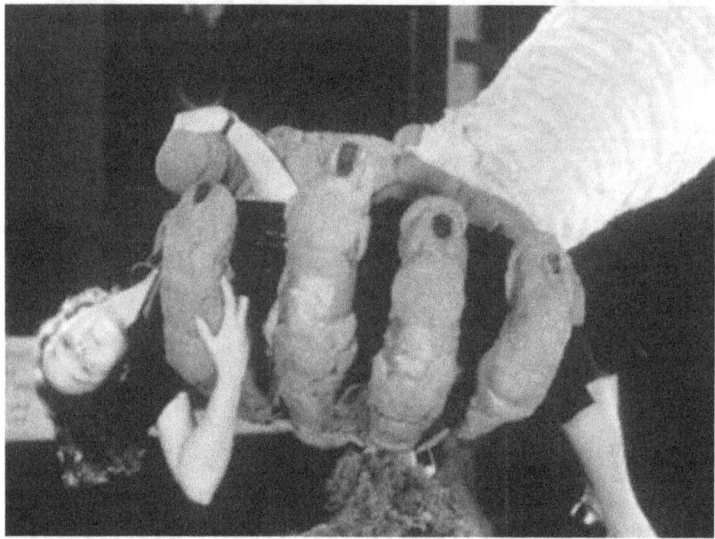

Cooper's secretary, Zoey Porter is reluctantly "volunteered" by her boss to be the first test victim of Delgado's fully articulated but incompletely furred and detailed hand

be the first to perform in a new and better articulated hand of Kong created for future scenes. Unlike the simpler prop used earlier, the new hand had a more realistically jointed thumb and stiff, adjustable finger joints, that allowed the hand to be "cupped" around Gertrude, holding her securely and safely in its grip. Delgado stated: "Somebody else did the first big hand, and it was used for a few shots, but it didn't 'cup' like a real hand, so I redesigned it."

Having abandoned earlier versions of the scene, both shot and written, Cooper would improvise over two days until he finally decided to haul her ignobly out of the room upside down. Another month went by and on December 9, Cooper directed Gertrude and Fay performing the exterior live-action shots outside the hotel window and above the city streets. The two actresses, starting with Gertrude, took turns performing in the improved hand before the rear screen projection of the New York streets far below. (Before the cameras began rolling, the ever-present, Edith Haskins acted as the stand-in for Fay and Gertrude.)

Starlet, Betty Furness was scheduled on the evening of that same day to portray the screaming woman in the window. The part was, instead, played by the RKO starlet, Sandra Shaw, the actress who would later, unknowingly, be credited as the "wrong woman." The future bride to the Prince of Hollywood, Gary Cooper, would be coached by her friend, Fay Wray, on how to scream: "Imagine that you have to get help from someone who's at least five blocks away. You've got to make them hear! Imagine!" By Sandra's own admission, "…she was so bad they even had to dub her scream."

Three days later, on December 13th, Gertrude's stunt double, Aline Goodwin, appeared in front of a similar rear screen projection, above the hotel street, for her turn in the new hand. Some of the finger joints at the bottom of the hand were strategically loosened to facilitate the fall. Hanging upside-down she covertly held on with her legs and hands until, cued by a twist and drop of the wrist, she was released to a soft landing below. Schoedsack stated that: "The hand that dropped the girl from the building was an articulated hand. The first one we had was just a ramrod affair that we shoved through the window."

Fay Wray wrote of her experience with the big hand in a September 21, 1969, *New York Times* article: "The hand and arm in which my close-up scenes were shot was about eight feet in length. Inside the furry arm, there was a steel bar, and the whole contraption (with me in the hand) could be raised or lowered like a crane. The fingers would be pressed around my waist while I was in a standing position. I would then be raised about ten feet into the air to be in line with an elevated camera. As I kicked and squirmed and struggled in the ape's hand, his fingers would gradually loosen and begin to open. My fear was real as I grabbed onto his wrist, his thumb, wherever I could, to keep from slipping out of that paw! When I could sense that the moment of minimum safety had arrived, I would call imploringly to the director and ask to be lowered to the floor of the stage. Happily, this was never denied for a second too long! I would have a few moments' rest, be re-secured in the paw, and the ordeal would begin all over again … a kind of pleasurable torment!"

So now we have the story … pleasurable torment. But we still don't have the answer. Why would the authors of *The Making of King Kong* misidentify Sandra Shaw as the "wrong woman?" Did Harriet have anything to do with it?

The book's co-author, George Turner, confessed he learned that Sandra Shaw was the "wrong woman" shortly after the first edition was published in 1975. This made it possible to check his facts and make corrections for the 1976 revised edition.

He didn't. Why?

George Turner was a

much loved and well-seasoned newsman and researcher who became an editor of *The American Cinematographer* magazine and resident historian of the American Society of Cinematographers. He was an expert on RKO. He knew classic films and *The Making of King Kong* was a lifelong passion project.

One of his contemporaries wrote: "The late George Turner was one of the most thorough film historians I ever met. I can't see him hearing something 'second-hand' without him doing a lot of research to verify someone else's recollection or a vague rumor about some one or some thing."

Yet, for unknown reasons, he stuck with his original 1976 source.

But Sandra was *not* the "wrong woman." So, who told him otherwise? And why did they lie or mislead George? What was their motive? What were they trying to hide? Did George know the truth? If so, then why would he lie? There were many still-surviving members of the cast and crew who would have known. Director, Ernest Schoedsack would have directed the scene. Ruth Rose, Schoedsack's wife and the screenwriter who wrote the scene, was on set every day to provide rewrites for the endless updating and improvising by directors.

Marcel Delgado and his brother helped build the full-size hand and head of Kong and would most likely have been on the set for their use during all the "wrong woman" shoots. And not only did Fay Wray perform before the same "EXTERIOR HOTEL-REAR SCREEN," on the same day that Gertrude Sutton performed her similar "wrong woman" scene, but she also, on the same evening, coached her friend, Sandra Shaw on how

The "wrong woman" scene from Kong's third draft screenplay titled *The Eighth Wonder* dated June 16, 1932. It was the last version of the script prior to Ruth Rose's treatment update to revise the "wrong woman" scene for Harriet Hagman. Written by James A. Creelman and based on Cooper's notes it conflates the "screaming woman" and the "wrong woman" while still very closely mirroring the finished scene in the movie. It was possibly the source for much of the promotional material regarding the "wrong woman" and other scenes released contemporaneously with the film. An exception was the *King Kong* novelization which used the Ruth Rose script for Harriet Hagman and was released two months prior to the film's release. *(Courtesy of UCLA Library Special Collections Performing Arts)*

to scream from the window. Surely one or more of these people knew the truth.

The Making of King Kong was revised two more times, in 2006 and 2018 without the record being corrected. So, who or what was behind this obfuscation of the truth?

Two different and widely separated actions skewed the future view of our story during its pass through the image altering, phantasmagoria machine of Hollywood. The first happened at the beginning of the wild rush into Kong's production, promotion, and release. The other was a Hollywood love story.

Kong's innovative, massive and unprecedented cross media campaign, used to promote this unique motion picture, included all media. Radio, newspapers (contests, puzzles, and comic strips), magazines, a novelization, billboards, sheet music, and film teasers would notify the public of something spectacular and completely different being offered by RKO Radio Pictures. New and unique promotional outlets and materials needed to be developed while the script and movie were still in the process of being simultaneously written and shot. As a consequence, sometimes preproduction artwork and scripts were used that presented an alternate take from the final film and elicited future confusion about a film most people remembered principally through the liberally recycled promotional materials.

Photographic innovations became necessary. In addition to the usual on-set photos of the actors performing, and in-studio photographic sessions with

These early promotional materials show, men devoured in a pit of giant spiders and vermin, a stegosaurus blocking the log bridge, and Kong escaping from the open, circus-like atmosphere of Madison Square Gardens instead of the confines of the Shrine Auditorium. These images would triumphantly announce *King Kong*'s release, but would never be seen by audiences in the finished film.

RKO used the standard method of in-studio photoshoots to create promotional materials. Cabot, Fay and Armstrong (top) "mug" for the studio camera. Cabot and Fay (bottom) confront the formidable studio camera, while Fay (right) cowers fetchingly for fans.

Another standard method was "posed on-set photos" of the actors re-enacting their scenes for the still photographer in between their film takes. (Opposite page, above & below)

the principles, some large format (A.K.A. hi-res) publicity photographs of the miniatures were prepared as a compositing source for large cut-and- paste promotional images depicting Kong in action.

But no additional promotional images of these kind would be generated that would highlight the "wrong woman." As was standard for all of Kong's special effects shoots, with the exception of a single unusable, lo-res "exposure test shot" of Harriet

Hagman, there were no live, on-set photos. With no additional promotional materials generated during or after Kong's production, the lack of information allowed ample room for misinterpretation and speculation about the "wrong woman" scene.

Of particular interest, and the source of some unexpected obfuscations over time can be exemplified in the contemporary recycling of Mystery Magazine's 1933 promotion of Kong. Janus Film's 1969

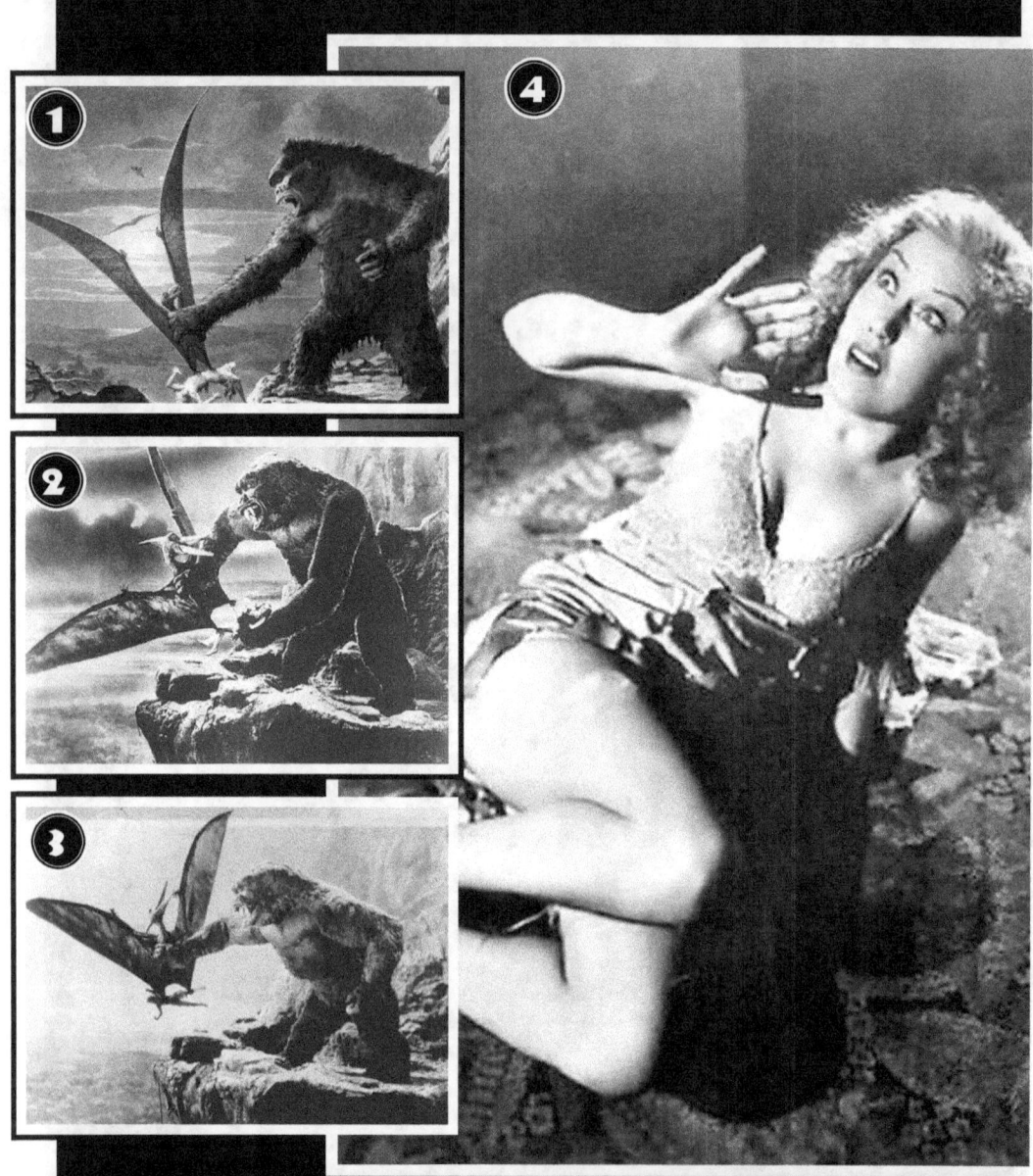

RKO had a problem. The most dramatic scenes in the film were of an animated Kong with real actors. But they were unusable for the mass mailing of high quality promotional photos to the press and theaters. Innovations became necessary.

These two series of sequences (both numbered (1) through (4) illustrate the "cut-and paste" process RKO developed to create the needed materials.

(1) They started with the artist rendering.

(2) They proposed creating a dramatic, cut-and-paste image.

(3) & (4) They used enlarged photos of miniature sets and creatures, and studio shots of posed actors to provide a source for the cutouts needed to prepare the paste-ups. Finally, the assembled cut-and-paste images would be touched up and photographed to provide a quality negative for mass production of promotional photos (2) that the publicity department would ship out to newspapers and theater owners.

Fay Wray catches up on the Kong story in *Mystery Magazine* while on the set in Kong promotional photo. The inaccurate Kong summary conflating the "wrong woman" and "the woman who screams from the hotel window" was reprinted in *Famous Monsters of Filmland* #27, March 1964 and #108 October 1974.

limited release screenings of the *restored print* of *King Kong that contained the "wrong woman" scene*, did not awaken fans to the existence of two distinctly different actresses in *King Kong's* "wrong woman" scene (nor were our victimized characters noticed in multiple home video releases of the restored version beginning 15 years later with the Criterion laserdisc release). They continued to lovingly hold in their memory the censored version they were familiar with. So, with the identification of Sandra as the "wrong woman" in 1976's *The Making of King Kong*, fans chose to continue to conflate the two actresses as one. They believed both were the formerly unknown and "unbilled" actress, Sandra Shaw.

This makes sense because the popular fan magazine, *Famous Monsters of Filmland*, also conflated the two women when they reprinted a detailed 1933 summary of *Kong* from *Mystery Magazine* in both their 1964 and 1974 issues. So, even before (and after) they saw the restored prints of *King Kong*, their favorite magazine unknowingly and

But the revolving doors which formed the entrance to the hotel were an effective barrier to the puzzled ape. They were too small for him to pass thru. Baffled, and jabbering with rage, he looked up at the tall structure that confronted him. A few floors above, a girl was near a window, wondering what was causing the commotion in the street.

To Kong this could be no one but Ann.

He reached up, grasped hold of the stone coping above and started to climb the building. The window ledges made convenient steps. He reached the girl's window, reached in and wrapped his big paw around her.

He gave her one glance and flung her back into the room, a look of disappointment on his face. Determinedly, he climbed from floor to floor, peering thru each window as he went.

In a behind-the-scenes publicity shot (left), Fay Wray and Producer Merian C. Cooper promote Mystery Magazine's inaccurate summary of King Kong that conflated the actresses (Sandra Shaw and Gertrude Sutton). In this Kong excerpt (right) from *Mystery Magazine*, the author conflates the "screaming woman" (she doesn't scream) and the "wrong woman" (she doesn't die) while loosely mirroring the finished scene in the movie.

incorrectly reached back to the deceptive apparitions of Hollywood's golden age to convince fans that the censored prints of Kong they had watched for years contained the first half of the "wrong woman" scene featuring Sandra Shaw as "the woman who screams from the window" and that Sandra Shaw was also the "wrong woman" cast to her death by Kong.

In contrast, the authors of *The Making of King Kong* never conflated the two actresses. They just misconstrued and mis-identified both of them. Their *unknown source* led them to believe that Sandra Shaw was the actress playing Kong's victim, the "wrong woman." She wasn't. That was Gertrude Sutton. It was also implied that they believed Sandra had been the first "wrong woman." She wasn't. That was Harriet. And they never identified who the unknown and unbilled actress portraying "the woman who screams from the window" was. Perhaps they didn't know. She actually *was* Sandra Shaw. But they never properly identified either actress. The fans of *Kong* and the authors of *The Making of King Kong* were laboring under two separate misperceptions, from two separate sources, spawned by and from the land of illusion, Hollywood, U.S.A.

But the authors, unlike

the fans, could more easily have known there were two different actresses in the film because they had their own *restored print* of *King Kong that contained the "wrong woman" scene*. And they frequently referred to it during the process of researching and writing the book and could easily have seen and known the two women were not the same actress.

By 1984 the fans had their own complete unedited version of the film with the release of the Criterion Special Edition laserdisc, and it was still another 35 years and multiple improved digital releases before they noticed there were two distinct actresses rather than one.

Perhaps, had the authors and fans looked with a critical eye, and without the "suspension of disbelief" usually surrendered for the enjoyment of this dream-like experience; had their acquiescence not allowed them to blend the two actresses as one, they might have unburdened themselves of their mistaken conflation of the two actresses. They may even have noticed and been able to identify Sandra Shaw as "the woman who screams from the window" rather than their mistaken belief she was the "wrong woman" who was being pulled from the window. But they didn't, and perhaps this altered state of mind shines a light on another answer requiring a wider perspective of the dream capital in its golden age.

Hollywood was, and is, a city of illusion. To experience its dreamscape, movie goers must "suspend their disbelief" and willingly let go of any critical focus. Critical gaze will tell us the extraordinary feats performed by the stars are, in actuality, multiple different stunt people and doubles and tricks of visual dexterity. Yet we willingly accept a 24-foot gorilla, that in reality is only 18 inches tall, could exist and knock airplanes out of the air from the top of the Empire State building. Yielding to the experience is the price of admission to the entertainment. But Hollywood, in its Golden Age, did not only manufacture illusions for the silver screen. Illusions were manufactured everywhere.

Tinseltown was really a small town under the intimidating control of the powerful, and all-encompassing iron hand of the studios. The control was necessary to meticulously maintain the star's manufactured personas to sustain their drawing power with the audience. To this end, the studios created a sophisticated disinformation campaign fed to the trade papers, the press, and the fan magazines through their publicity department. An alternate reality with new names and enhanced, false biographies and rumors of wealth, beauty, romance, and adventure were proliferated to a willing public hungry for distraction. The public willingly supplied their "suspension of disbelief" to this extended canvas for the meager price of uplifting mundane lives. The larger-than-life image of the star on the screen was blended with the persona of the real personality.

Truth and myth were inextricably bound together, conflated by a 24/7 phantasmagoria

Rocky and Gary Cooper hanging with her aunt, Delores del Rio, at Uncle Cedric Gibbons estate, a center of Hollywood society.

machine weaving its mythical magic into the very fabric of what Hollywood was. Into this miasma of floating fantasy was enacted a marriage between the lovers, movie star Gary Cooper and his bride, the socialite, Veronica Balfe, who as a budding RKO starlet had become Sandra Shaw. The authors and/or "their sources" chose to characterize this marriage in a seriously misleading and meager reductive form when they wrote: *"The unbilled actress who so effectively portrayed the victim was Sandra Shaw, then 19, wife-to-be of Gary Cooper."*

The subtext of this statement sparked and encouraged some distorted Hollywood flourishes born in the long-lasting and more restrictive Breen Production Code era, initiated a year after their marriage and the release of *King Kong*. The abbreviated suggestion, knowingly or unknowingly, insinuated a Cinderella-like story of a struggling young starlet marrying a prince of Hollywood who was thus anointed a princess of the land. But the intimation runs counter to the facts. True, in 1933 Gary Cooper was a star and, though not yet the icon of Hollywood royalty he would become, he was an unofficial "Prince of Hollywood."

But Sandra Shaw, before being illuminated by the glaring publicity of Cooper and Kong's starlight, was more than a struggling "unbilled" actress. She was, in actuality, socialite Veronica Balfe.

More a princess than a Cinderella, she was the stepdaughter of the governor of the New York Stock Exchange; her uncle was Cedric Gibbons, the most famous art director in Hollywood history and a founder of the Academy of Motion Pictures Arts and Sciences. Her aunt, by marriage to Gibbons, was the beautiful film star, Mexican aristocrat, and Hollywood socialite, Delores Del Rio.

Sandra Shaw, the budding actress contracted to RKO, was more a fanciful mirage, a lark for a wealthy young socialite, than fact. Her predecessors to the title of the "wrong woman," Gertrude Sutton and Harriet Hagman had retained their real names. Veronica, instead, assumed a fake Hollywood moniker, not for the usual purpose of enhancing her image but to obfuscate it and transform it into an entity of the Hollywood dream machine.

Veronica, or "Rocky," as she was known to her friends, was a true debutante who had been formally presented to New York society just two years before. When the 31-year-old Cooper met the striking 19-year-old beauty at her uncle's societal gathering for an Easter Sunday party, he was struck by the self-possession and composure in one so young.

Cooper was a still rising star, best known for his good looks and simple cowboy-like manner. (NOTE: Fay Wray and Gary Cooper were close friends back to the silent era when Paramount unsuccessfully promoted them as a couple in several films. Gary would be best man at her 1928 marriage to John Monk Saunders.)

Old pals Gary Cooper and Fay Wray make fun of their images at a Hollywood costume party, late in 1933. Miss Shaw (unseen here), dressed as her aunt Delores del Rio in *Bird of Paradise*, passed completely under the radar at the party, even though Gary was formally courting her at the time. The event also included Mr. and Mrs. David O. Selznick, Merian C. Cooper, and Gary's former paramour (and no friend of Rocky's), socialite Countess di Frasso.

Despite Cooper's image as the shy and haltingly awkward speaker, he had a beautiful, well-trained, and cultured speaking voice. But he would always default to his screen persona when near a camera, a microphone, or at a public event.

He was also an enthusiastic and committed social

climber who enjoyed living the aristocratic life of a socialite. He had sought it out and been introduced into its inner circles through his extended affair with the older, scandalous, and married, Countess di Frasso. The end of this affair and Coop's marriage to "Rocky" cemented his place in polite society.

The upper classes, for centuries, had been navigating the societal minefield of social polarization that would feel familiar to a star from the kingdom of Hollywood in the 1930s. The sophisticated traditions of this aristocratic lifestyle had appealed to "Coop." The cultured style offered him a country gentleman persona, as well as the understanding and tolerance of his societal peers for his many affairs over the years. (Coop's director, Stuart Heisler, said that: "Coop was probably the greatest cocksman that ever lived." A moniker he could have shared with his wife's uncle and Hollywood socialite, Cedric Gibbons.)

As the stricter, conservative-Catholic-driven Breen Production Code forced a greater and greater separation and conflict between Coop's public and private persona, this accommodation with polite society helped him salve the psychic wounds his Hollywood lifestyle inflicted. He was able to survive and navigate the stresses of an unnatural, and nearly impossible, embodiment of a schizophrenic fabrication imposed on a star by a studio system that promoted and sold it to the public during Tinseltown's golden age. His ordination into international society through his marriage to "Rocky" saved him and had as much or more to do with making Cooper a prince than he had to do with making her a princess.

This, too, is a Hollywood story…

We can be clear what the authors' of TMoKK intentions were. They assumed the readers, like themselves, would accept this flourish of Hollywood distortion … Sandra Shaw, whose name was conjured in Hollywood, was a lucky girl who became a princess.

But this leading and understated blandishment hid the truth for 42 years. Gary Cooper was the magic portal … the hypnotic suggestion calling up a remnant of a story told long ago. His portal grants access to the Hollywood dream state and in our own willing "suspension of disbelief" we respond to the shared myths rather than our own critical gaze. Hollywood fiction became truth, and this fanciful anecdote of Sandra Shaw was just another manufactured dream. But it was a Hollywood story that was a far cry from the true Hollywood stories of her sisters in struggle.

So, we come full circle: Why Sandra Shaw? Well… First, we must understand that there is confusion about the identity of the "wrong woman" that does not originate with Sandra Shaw. There are misunderstandings that result from a continuous confusion between, and about, the identities of the three women associated with the *wrong woman.* Even in the two separate issues of *Famous Monsters of Filmland* containing the Kong summary, the editors were confused about who the *wrong woman* was. They printed the only existing photo of Hagman as the *wrong woman*. Yet in two different captions, in their two different issues, they give two different, conflicting, and confusing descriptions. In the 1964 caption of the photo of Harriet in Kong's hand they mistakenly state, "as seen on the screen." But Harriet was never seen on the screen. That was Gertrude. They appear to have mistaken the blond Harriet for Fay Wray. The 1974 caption reads: "Kong's hand goes into action as he grasps *wrong girl* in New York bedroom, mistaking her for Ann Darrow." They were the first to identify her as the "wrong girl." But the "wrong girl" in the photo is a *blonde* Harriet Hagman, and not the *brunette* Gertrude Sutton who was in the finished film. The entire backstory of the "wrong woman" is, at best, inconsistent, obscure, or nonexistent in any and all follow-up publications.

Kong's production, intentionally or not, supplied very little clear information about these actresses. So, what do we know? We know Harriet Hagman was initially intended to be remembered when Selznick chose to promote her with a featured role as the "wrong woman." This changed when she became an uncomfortable truth that Selznick and Cooper preferred to go unnoticed and forgotten. The uncredited "bit player," Gertrude

Harriet is held in the full-sized hand of Kong in the only known photo existing (likely a photographic exposure test) of her performance (from the private collection of Kong's special effects wizard, Willis O'Brien). The position of Harriet's legs indicates she is seated on a support inside the hand that faces her toward the exit window at screen left, she has twisted around to face the camera.

Sutton was never meant to be remembered. And though Cooper likely facilitated a few "bit parts" for her in 1933 (including in the Kong sequel, *Son of Kong*), she never advanced beyond minor or uncredited parts, including her last role in 1944. Sandra Shaw was also not intended to be remembered. But the hungry specters of the Hollywood dream machine had showered her with stardust when she had later married Gary Cooper and his starlight pulled her into its distorted magical mirror. She would be seen through the portal of Cooper's powerful stardom. So, she became the Cinderella story of an obscure, struggling, and "unbilled" actress who married a prince of Hollywood and became a princess.

But who would have motive to falsely name Sandra Shaw as the "wrong woman" or, perhaps to obscure the identities of Harriet Hagman and Gertrude Sutton? A basic truth is that nothing happens in a vacuum. Rumor and drama are always with us, especially on a film set where rumor and drama are baked into the job. RKO was a pressure cooker as the official launch of Kong's production approached and many motives pushing in contradictory directions and at cross purposes with one another emerged. Careers, egos, and a real threat to the existence of RKO as a company were being tested and weighed in the balance.

'King Kong and the Wrong Woman' continues on the following page.

" **… Now he comes to civilization merely a captive … a show to gratify your curiosity."**
— *Carl Denham*

KING KONG

PART FOUR: CONCLUSION: A CLOSER LOOK

It may help us to take another closer look at the Harriet Hagman shoot and the milieu of personalities and motives that initiated and drove its production. Because the "wrong woman" scene was of current and topical interest during the writing of TMoKK, and, having read Ruth Rose's script, its authors were aware an alternate scene had been shot. They would likely have asked some of Kong's principalss about it. Yet the book's only commentary reads:

"The large head proved unsatisfactory for these scenes because it was too inflexible to convey the idea the ape was hanging onto

The "long face" Kong (left) had more human dimensions. The "round face" Kong (right) was more ape-like and preferred by Cooper. (Note: Because the Kong models needed to be resculpted and repaired on a daily basis, alterations and inconsistencies were inevitable.)

the side of the building and moving about."

This analysis places all the blame for the failure of the scene on the "big head," rather than the personalities involved in the production and there is no mention of a different actress portraying the "wrong woman." In fact, there is no mention of the source of the statement.

The commentary could have been sourced from anyone involved in shooting or editing of the scene. But it suggests intimate knowledge of the shoot and suggests a consensus opinion was reached quickly (probably during the shoot) and the "creator and boss," Cooper, who had suggested the use of the "big head" in the first

place, had reached this same conclusion. But Cooper did not immediately act on this consensus. He waited another month before shooting the similar Fay Wray scene and another two months before surreptitiously putting Gertrude Sutton before the cameras.

There were fundamental differences about how Kong should be portrayed even before a frame of the New York "test film" was shot. Obie insisted the audience could not sympathize with a character that was just a beast. But Cooper wanted his "terror gorilla." So, Obie counterpunched and had Delgado build a "half-ape, half-human" animation model to more

human dimensions, with shorter arms and a longer spine. Cooper responded with a jab: "That's the funniest thing I've ever seen."

Obie took another couple shots, allowing some more ape-like features until Cooper was fed up with the skirmish; "I want…the fiercest, most brutal, monstrous damned thing that has ever been seen. I'll have women crying over him before I'm through, and the more brutal he is the more they'll cry at the end." Then he made a referee call. He presented Obie with the precise measurements of a male bull gorilla proclaiming, "Now, that's what I want."

"Obie was a tough guy too," said Goldner. The

hard-drinking Irishman announced his resignation and swaggered to his neutral corner, the local speakeasy, to grouse. But he came back and built the new armature with longer arms, a shorter spine, and a simian visage as per Cooper's specifications.

While the new Kong was being built, the necessity to begin shooting the "test film" meant putting a more ape-like face and covering on Obie's existing human-like armature (that the fans dubbed "long face") until Cooper's model with the dimensions of a male bull gorilla, a fuller face and a larger, more prominent simian-like brow (dubbed "round face" by the fans) could be completed for use in finishing the majority of the filming. (The mind's natural tendency to impress consistency on action means that the average audience member doesn't notice the dissimilarities in the different models. This same tendency allowed Cooper to play fast and loose with the size of Kong whose apparent height alternated from 18 to 60 feet tall during the film.)

Cooper and Obie were both of a pugnacious nature

and this would not be their last confrontation. But Cooper respected people who stood up for themselves and, in the end, he got his "terror gorilla" and Obie still managed to infuse a child-like humanity into a lifeless hunk of rubber, cotton, and metal.

Obie was probably on-set for all the "wrong woman" shoots, and he was the only one who kept a photo of Harriet Hagman as the "wrong woman." Had his widow not supplied *Famous Monsters of Filmland* magazine with this singular image and the information that it was a picture of the "wrong girl," (Obie often made notes on the back of his photos) this article would not have been initiated. Without this information, Harriet would probably not have been discovered. Obie had been a boxer. He would have been pleased he got in the last jab.

It was a big day. Finally, they had the full financial backing of the studio. It was a day of triumph, the official start of production. Everyone would have been there: Cooper to oversee the first day of shooting, Schoedsack directed, and Ruth

Rose was there for rewrites if needed. Obie and Vernon Walker (Head of Camera Effects Department) always oversaw the rear screen shots, and there would be additional personnel to operate the rear screen projector, and the "big hand" as well as the usual camera, lighting and set crew, and assistants for Cooper, Schoedsack, etc. It probably was not a good idea to begin production with a complex effects shot. First day shoots are usually about establishing a successful routine. Setting up and synchronizing large props, actors, and rear screen projection is a challenging endeavor to say the least. But, switching to a new and different, untried effects prop in mid-shoot is an even worse idea. They must have been feeling cocky.

From his very first proposal to Selznick about making *King Kong*, Cooper had stated, "The results of animation show that the animals will always be somewhat mechanical (and) ... with close-up work of *full-sized head* mask and hands and feet... should prove

In this scene from the "test film," (on the left) Cooper replaced this close-up of Kong, reaching for Fay Wray beneath the fallen tree with a close-up of the "big head" (on the right). Cooper later enjoyed getting Marcel Delgado to admit, at a screening of the film, that the "big head" was effective. He also replaced a close-up shot of the "long faced" Kong roaring at the sailors on the log with an improved close-up of the "round faced" Kong.

sensational." He always intended to make a large head for close-ups of his monster ape for a more dramatic effect. And yet, Cooper had, instead, made allowance for Harriet's scene to use a rear screen projection of the animated Kong behind the hotel window.

Then, apparently, Cooper decided the animated shots of Kong were unsatisfactory. It's even possible Obie may have delivered a rear screen projection of Cooper's least favorite, "long-faced" Kong. (Note: Over the course of production, Cooper developed a general dissatisfaction with the look of Kong's initial animation model close-ups; his only choice while shooting the "test film." During the subsequent editing he removed or replaced them with improved close-ups of either his preferred, "round-faced" animation model or the "big head"). But this time Cooper had his newly completed "big head" so he had a choice. He opted to make this the tryout for his shiny new, full-size prop.

It turned out to be a bad call on multiple levels. The failure of the "big head" gave support to those who were questioning the viability of a project that could still fall apart. The film could still be halted before any real money was spent. Once again Cooper and Selznick were barraged with panicked calls about possible runaway costs. It also deprived Selznick of an opportunity to promote his starlet, who would be scapegoated and let go. And then there was Harriet who would lose her opportunity at the spotlight and a career. Cooper's fancy footwork would allow him to skirt disaster and give him a path to return to his original preferred wrong woman concept. But it was a costly victory and not one he would want to brag about.

A further fly in the ointment was that the founding father of the most sophisticated techniques in the field of miniatures and stop-motion animation may have

KONG / 116

arms the body of a woman. This motif symbolizes the
story as adapted for the screen. Marcel Delgado made
some of the special properties, such as dessicated human
heads mounted on plaques or floating in jars of
embalming fluid.

By the time The Most Dangerous Game was in the
can, Kong, despite the secrecy surrounding it, was the
talk of the studios. The test reel, consisting of
approximately ten minutes of outrageous but enthralling
action, was calculated to make the viewer want more.
A dozen large illustrations, ranging from fifteen to
twenty-one inches in width, served to demonstrate the
highlights planned for the feature. Larrinaga and Crabbe
rendered these scenes intricately in carbon pencil after
O'Brien's rough sketches. Cooper unveiled the drawings
to the studio's board of directors when the test was
screened. Most were used in the final production:

(1) A brontosaurus rises from the water,
capsizing a lifeboat containing Ann Darrow, the male
leads and several sailors; (2) Kong carries Ann through
the jungle toward a chasm bridged by a gigantic log; (3)
Kong shakes the log, tumbling sailors into the chasm;

Page from the rough manuscript of *The Making of King Kong*, typed by George Turner, with notes in the margins by Orville Goldner.

All the King's Men, Douglas Turner's 2011 book on Kong.

Kong would express Obie's dissatisfaction with production disputes by having Kong "whip the bird" or "crap in the woods."). But Obie died in 1962; too early to supply George Turner with information in 1976.

The principals listed as contributors to *The Making of King Kong* were still subject to the same ongoing Hollywood distortions. Very few of these principalss would know many or most of the interconnecting detail from the film set to the boardrooms of New York and L.A. Any gaps in their information allowed room for rumor and Hollywood flourishes to lose or distort the truth. It's not even an unreasonable assumption that TMoKK author, and Kong miniatures technician, Orville Goldner, and/ or any number of other surviving crew members, could have passed on an unsubstantiated rumor about Sandra Shaw's role in the "wrong woman" shoot if they'd had only sporadic connection to any of the filming.

been offended, not only by the rejection of his rear screen animation footage, but also by Cooper's brash action leading to the ineffective and inappropriate use of the "big head." Obie had been upfront about his preference for using animation over the "big head." He could only hope Cooper would be chastened and more careful about its future use.

He would have been happy Cooper had to reshoot with the animated Kong in the window. And probably not completely unhappy to see Cooper suffer the eating-of-crow over the "big head" failure. Still, this does not supply motive to misidentify Sandra Shaw except as a misdirected, humorous jab of rebellion (Subtle acts of chicanery often appeared in the filmed "dailies." When the day's animation was screened,

In his own book on Kong, *All the King's Men*,

Douglas Turner wrote about his father's journalistic quest through, *The Making of King Kong*, stating: "Because Goldner was a co-author on the book, he was never quoted directly. His words were paraphrased and often his experiences were rendered anonymous… The actual writing was mostly done by (George) Turner, but with many revisions, corrections and suggestions from Goldner." This makes Goldner appear as a likely source of the misinformation on Sandra Shaw. However, he continues with, "(Information was) culled from multiple conversations — both person to person and over the phone — as well as a long- running correspondence and notes in the margins of rough manuscript drafts of *The Making of King Kong*… over the course of several years from 1969 to 1976." This leads us back to the challenge of multiple suspects.

Of all the contributors to *The Making of King Kong* only Cooper would have known everything. He was a very hands-on producer, passionately involved in every detail of production (including publicity after Selznick's departure). He chose all the talent. He was also socially close and friendly with all the principals, including Selznick, Fay Wray, and Sandra Shaw. He was present for all the "wrong woman" shoots. Though there is no evidence that he ever directly interfered with the promotion of the "wrong woman" scene after removing Harriet from the role, the publicity department, oddly, generated three different printed versions for the public that undoubtedly only enhanced the confusion. And other than David O. Selznick, who passed away in 1965, he was the only one with a possible motive that might influence him to shy away from or shroud the full backstory of the "wrong woman." (It should be noted that Cooper was proud of the finished scene and was angry when he found out years later that the "wrong woman" had been censored with other scenes in 1938.) If Cooper was ever confronted with the question of the "wrong woman," he certainly made no effort to clarify the situation.

It is worth pointing out how personally identified Cooper and his story team were to this film; how closely they reflected and embodied Kong's main characters. When Ruth Rose assumed responsibility for the final script, Cooper told her to "put us in it… Make it a real Cooper/ Schoedsack expedition." And she did. Cooper became Carl Denham, the showman adventurer and sometimes he was his other self-proclaimed alter ego, *King Kong*. Schoedsack became Jack Driscoll, the woman hating adventurer with a soft heart of gold, and Ruth Rose, like Ann Darrow, had fallen in love with Monty Schoedsack on a shipboard expedition of exploration and adventure. Essentially, the three principal performers, were written, chosen, and directed by their own real-life counterparts.

The production of Kong was a difficult, passionate, and career defining experience for Cooper, and he could be defensive when responding to criticism and commentary on his uniquely personal film. He was known for the periodic

(Clockwise from left) The lovers, Monty Schoedsack and Ruth Rose. The visionary and showman, Merian C Cooper. And their counterparts, Jack Driscoll, Ann Darrow, and Carl Denham; the three Ds of their filmmaking motto, "Distant, Difficult, and Dangerous."

explosion of a fiery temper and it appears the Harriet Hagman blunder may have contained an uncomfortable memory of a stressful and awkward start of production to his signature film that he would prefer not to revisit. On the first shoot, he made a wrong call at the wrong time to exploit the "big head" against the advice of his effects team. Though he may have been unhappy with Obie's rear screen footage, there was no one to blame but himself for the near fiasco, except maybe Selznick. Cooper loved to tell the story that his number one supporter, Selznick, never interfered with his production of Kong. But there is little doubt that Selznick had pushed for the Harriet promotion with the official start of Kong's production at the same time his new contract negotiations began.

Selznick was trying to convince RKO to make more quality films with bigger budgets and RKO wanted budgets slashed across the board on his full roster of films. He would've seen this enhancement of his starlet to a more prominent role as good for the picture and for him. Cooper had liked Selznick's earlier suggestions for the newly contracted, Bruce Cabot and Cooper's highest paid actor, RKO contract player, Bob Armstrong. But not having his choice of actress and, at the same time, being required to alter the "wrong woman's" character was probably not as well received. The "wrong woman" scene was one of the earliest images Cooper promoted. It was among twelve promotional drawings prepared and presented to New York to promote the initial "test film" and to Edgar Wallace for the initial draft of the script. Selznick was intruding on his creative authority; interfering with his picture for what would appear to be an improvement in his negotiating position.

This sudden uncharacteristic interference, just as full production was greenlit, may have "got his temper up." Cooper may have felt Selznick's support was slipping. A man of such fierce loyalties as Cooper may very likely have felt some sting of betrayal from his cohort and

friend (as he would a few months later when Selznick deserted RKO for MGM). Also, because it was Selznick's idea, Cooper could see this as a spectre of future intrusions that could result from efforts to mollify New York that Cooper would not want to see repeated.

But this was only the beginning of New York's efforts to interfere with his film, which included a refusal to pay for an original score for Kong. After Cooper's ascendancy to Head of Production at RKO, President B. B. Kahane told composer Max Steiner to use some music tracks we already have." Steiner cried, "Old music tracks! For God's sake, Ben, what am I gonna use – music from *LITTLE WOMEN*?" Cooper would not and could not argue or afford to wait. Cooper was a warrior who had fought in the Great War. A stalled campaign was death on the battlefield and to stall the production at this point would be failure. For Kong to fulfill his vision he had to push forward. So, he paid for the groundbreaking score himself.

I'm not sure I can blame

the authors of *The Making of King Kong* for embracing the humble Cinderella-like story they had inherited. It really wasn't core to the main story they were telling. But it was "so Hollywood" and had so fortuitously been dropped right in their laps like a forty-year-old Easter egg from a Gilded Age, still dripping with the counterfeit Hollywood glitter of another time. The tale was irresistible, and the authors stayed with it through multiple printings and updates to their book and onto their passing without disclosing or noticing or crediting the misinformation or its source.

It should be noted that Cooper died in 1973, so he could not have supplied Sandra Shaw's name in 1976 when George received it.

Though we have tantalizing facts, there is still uncertainty as to the specific source of the muddied waters. Our suppositions have unearthed provocative hints about the possible suspects and it appears there is no lack of motivation among our players to leave the answers to these questions vague or unanswered. But the fully unveiled clarifying statement of truth we seek that would identify the culprit, or culprits who provided the attempted "coup de grâce" to Gertrude Sutton's performance for 43 years, still eludes us; hidden in some yet-to-be-discovered declaration or whispered suggestion recorded in some unknown text or image.

As intriguing as our surmises about the motives of Cooper and others may be, they represent only circumstantial evidence. We may still not be sure who named Sandra Shaw as the "wrong woman" or what their considerations may have been. You may still have to discover these yourself, hidden in the stories and suggestions I've shared or somewhere between the lines of your own dreamscape.

With deftly dancing images, unrooted in time and space, the silver screen mimics our dreams as written with the pen of our desires. Hollywood's shadowy images emulate the language our mind uses to impact us and fill our mental screens with the stories we tell ourselves. Because Hollywood is the land of stories, illusions, and desire, the truth may be hard to find. In a place where truth lies hidden beneath a blanket of dreams manufactured to comfort, titillate, or frighten us, it is prudent to recall their source and remember this … Though "We are the stories we are told, and the stories we tell ourselves," Hollywood is our master storyteller. ∎

ADDENDUM TO 'KING KONG AND THE WRONG WOMAN'

BY BART PIERCE

1) Fay Wray ran as far away as she could from her scream queen image until she finally embraced it many years later. The highlight of her obituary was her role as beauty opposite *King Kong*'s, beast. On August 10, 2003, two days after her passing, the Empire State Building dimmed its lights for fifteen minutes in honor of the star who had helped make it immortal.

2) Robert Armstrong begged Cooper to not make him say, "It was beauty killed the beast." But he would always be remembered as *King Kong*'s costar before and after his passing in 1973.

3) Bruce Cabot had a long career but the first paragraph, if not the first line, or headline announcing his death would be a remembrance of his role as the heroic Jack Driscoll in *King Kong*.

4) Willis O'Brien: Kong's special effects development during Obie's tenure transformed the industry. Marcel Delgado, Obie's model maker, referred to him as "the master." Cooper always insisted he was a genius. But at the end of 1933, the year of Obie's greatest triumph, his estranged, mentally ill wife shot and killed their two sons and herself. His was a childlike intellect. He suffered from alcoholism and struggled all his life, unsuccessfully, to surpass *King Kong*. He never did. In 1949, under producer Merian C. Cooper, he won the Academy Award for his effects in the film of Kong's, poor cousin, *Mighty Joe Young*. Upon his death the press declared: "*King Kong*'s Creator Dies"

5) Max Steiner was inspired by Kong to write a score that ignited him into a career for which he would be remembered as the father of motion picture music. In *King Kong* he set the standard for motion picture films that continues to this day.

6) David O. Selznick never matched his success in *Gone with the Wind*. He became enamored of cocaine and married a star he developed, Jennifer Jones. Though he made many more great pictures, he later specialized in discovering and developing a stable of stars he put under contract and leased out at high fees.

He'd asked Merian Cooper for a credit on Kong and got Executive Producer. But Selznick later wrote, "The picture was primarily by Cooper and Schoedsack, under my guidance; and one of the biggest gambles I took at RKO was to squeeze money out of the budgets of other pictures for this venture." Cooper later credited Selznick for his help, saying Kong would not have been possible without him. *King Kong* still remains on Selznick's impressive list of accomplishments.

7) Ruth Rose and Ernest "Monty" Schoedsack began their adventure when smitten on a high sea voyage of exploration that inspired the lead characters of *King Kong*. Together they were essential in the launch of a mythic tale of love and adventure that would long outlive them. They continued as a cinematic team until 1949; *Mighty Joe Young*, an echo of their first project together was their last film due to an accident in WWII during an upper atmosphere test of photo equipment that damaged Monty's eyesight. Rose and Monty retired to a quiet life until her passing in 1978 followed soon after by his passing in 1979. Their story had begun with love at first sight and had completed with their interment together. A highlight in their bios is their collaboration on *King Kong*.

8) Merian C. Cooper: After Kong and a stint as production head of RKO, Cooper successfully promoted Technicolor before returning to the romance of a justifiable war as the indispensable Chief of Staff to General Chennault's The Flying Tigers in World War II China. Exiting the war as a Brigadier General, his early experiences in revolutionary Russia inspired him with the necessity of countering communist propaganda by promoting American values in a series of inspiring films he co-produced with John Ford about the American West. In 1960, he received a special Technical Academy award for his support of industry-altering innovative achievements like Technicolor and the widescreen process, Cinerama. Like his Merlin, Willis O'Brien, his obituary proclaimed, "*King Kong*'s Creator Dies."

9) Cooper and Schoedsack both found their own Ann Darrows, in Dorothy Jordan and Ruth Rose, to love, support and share their lives.

10) Harriet Hagman, a survivor, gave up show business. She stood up for herself and divorced her lieutenant when he blackened both her eyes and put her in the hospital. Two more marriages resulted in finding the one with whom she shared the rest of her long life.

11) Gertrude Sutton lived and shared a fruitful life with her second partner.

12) Sandra Shaw (A.K.A. Veronica Balfe) shared a loving marriage with Gary Cooper, despite his many indiscretions. After his death, she married a successful plastic surgeon and continued a full life as a noted athlete, competing in golf, swimming, scuba diving, surfing, and tennis, and she was named California's female skeet champion.

13) All three of our "wrong women" lived long, full, and interesting lives. No mention of *King Kong* appeared in any of their obituaries.

14) *King Kong* continues to this day as a multimillion-dollar franchise. ∎

SON OF KONG
and the
Uncredited Star

by DAVID GOUDSWARD

In 1933, nine months after the success of a little film called *King Kong*, RKO Pictures released *Son of Kong*.

In the sequel, filmmaker Carl Denham is broke. Blamed for the destruction caused by Kong in New York, he hides in his boarding house. His landlady can barely keep the process servers outside and away from him. He leaves New York by freighter and ends up back on Skull Island.

The landlady was played by actress Kathrin Clare Ward, born in Bradford as Katie Clare O'Connor on November 2, 1871, the fifth child of Irish immigrants James and Catherine (Welch) O'Connor, who worked in the shoe industry.

Ward probably didn't move to Tinsel Town looking to be a movie star. It was the mid-1920s. Talking pictures were still experimental.

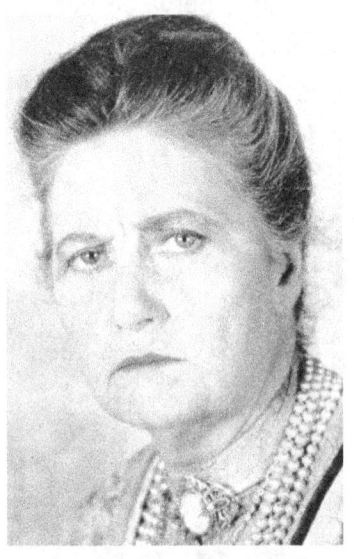

Kathrin Clare Ward

Al Jolson's *Jazz Singer,* the first feature-length motion picture with sound, would not appear until 1927. And as a solidly built Irish-woman in her 50s, Ward knew she was no longer leading lady material.

As a child, she saw her older siblings leaving school to work. In the 1880 census, her 16, 14, and 12-year-old brother and sisters were already working in a hat shop.

As soon as she turned 21, Katie fled Haverhill to avoid the factory life of her family. She moved to Boston and used her remarkable voice and a memorized repertoire of Irish songs to make a living. There is no record of Katie ever returning to Haverhill. Her parents were dead by 1907, and with the Catholic Church's opinion of theater people, it was unlikely she would have been welcomed home.

By the late 1890s, she had moved to New York City with a thriving career in nightclubs and private events. As Katherine Klare, she parlayed that into a popular member of a musical comedy troupe. An interview at the beginning of the 1905 season noted that she had decided to join the vaudeville circuit in 1906.

New York City was dismayed but not surprised. Vaudeville was the logical next step for a rising show business career. She quickly graduated to a headliner on the vaudeville circuits, singing Irish songs as Katherine Klare, the "Irish Thrush." Several newspaper reviews considered "the new Maggie Cline," Haverhill's other successful Irish chanteuse. There's no record of how Maggie Cline felt about the description, considering Cline didn't retire until 1917.

In 1914, Katherine O'Connor married another singer on the circuit, Charles B. Ward, between performances in Chicago. She and Ward performed together intermittently as they toured with different companies. Ward not only wrote his own songs, he also owned New-York Music Company. This publishing house printed and distributed sheet music, his in particular. His most famous song was "The Band Played On," which everyone knows by the opening lines. "Casey would waltz with a strawberry blonde."

The Wards continued to tour but were starting to prefer West Coast circuits. The "Irish Thrush" expanded appearances to include light opera. The Wards were soon living in San Francisco, touring only locally.

When Ward died in 1917, Katherine Clair Ward was ensconced in San Francisco society. She had a steady income thanks to the publishing company residuals, and she dabbled in local theater but soon grew bored. Within a decade, she decided on the move to Hollywood.

Hollywood appealed to Ward because, after decades of touring the vaudeville and burlesque circuits, she knew everyone. All the

Son of Kong promised much, but many critics and moviegoers felt it didn't live up to its namesake.

actors and crew who saw vaudeville dying as films took over went to California to try their luck.

She didn't need the money, but to break the tedium and see old friends, she became a "six-liner," a bit player hired for one day and usually had less than six speaking lines. She launched a new career playing landladies, mothers-in-law, and hired help. Having an Irish accent she could switch on and off helped. Most of the time, the roles were uncredited, which was the norm. Even her part in *Son of Kong*, which had more than six lines, was uncredited.

Kathrin Clare Ward was her stage name in the agency casting catalogs, but her credited roles were few, so she may have used several version before settling on her final choice. She appeared as Katherine Ward, Katherine Clair Ward, and Katherin Ward, as well as Kathrin Clare Ward. Kathrin Clare Ward was also the one on her obituary, so the other variations may have been studios not particularly concerned about the bit players.

She may not have cared. In 1929, now that there was sound, her late husband's songs started appearing in movies. A percentage of each use came to her via the music company. Kathrin Clare Ward was never in danger of being a starving artist in Hollywood.

She died on October 14, 1938, in Los Angeles, California, USA, having appeared in five films the year before. She was 67 and had performed for 46 of those years. Her brief obituary in the *Los Angeles Times* notes her death "removed another veteran from theatrical ranks."

During her film career, she appeared as an extra in films starring fellow ex-vaudevillians like Will Rogers, Mae West, Joe E. Brown, and Olsen & Johnson. She worked with directors such as Busby Berkeley, Cecil B. DeMille, Mack Sennett, and D. W. Griffith. ∎

An earlier version of this article ran as "Haverhill's Forgotten Movie Star" in Wavelengths – the Newsletter of WHAV 97.9 FM & WHAV.net. Used with permission.

DEAD MAN'S BRAND
Norbert Davis

I first encountered the work of Norbert Davis in Ron Goulart's anthology *The Hardboiled Dicks* (one of the most important and influential anthologies of

NORBERT DAVIS

DEAD MAN'S BRAND

AND OTHER TALES OF THE OLD WEST

With an introduction by Spur Award winner
BILL PRONZINI

Art: Tom Roberts

the past fifty years, if you ask me), which included a story featuring Davis's private eye character Max Latin, "Don't Give Your Right Name."

Great stuff, and since then I've read many other pulp mystery stories by Davis. He's probably best known for his trio of novels featuring a PI named Doan and a Great Dane known as Carstairs.

I knew Davis had written other things besides mysteries, but I wasn't really aware he had done Westerns until Tom Roberts of Black Dog Books published *Dead Man's Brand*, a collection of eight of Davis's stories from various Western pulps. (And that's Tom's artwork on the cover, by the way.) As you might expect if you're familiar with Davis's work, they're all top-notch yarns.

"A Gunsmoke Case for Major Cain" (*Dime Western*, October 1940) is a frontier legal thriller with an exciting courtroom scene and a neat twist. It was also Davis's

(Continued on page 162)

King Kong and Me

By WILL MURRAY

King Kong and I go back a long way. More than 60 years ago, I was first mesmerized by the colossal ape with the too-human eyes due to a Saturday afternoon Creature Feature television broadcast of the RKO film of 1933 when I was growing up in the early 1960s. I rewatched *King Kong* whenever it came on. So I was quite familiar with the beast-god of Skull Island when I picked up the 1964 issue of *Famous Monsters of Filmland* with a King Kong "Special Photo Filmbook" cover feature, and built the Kong Aurora monster model kit that

(Continued on next page)

BY
WILL MURRAY

Doc Savage and *King Kong* circa 1964 — both reprinted by Bantam Books, and both illustrated by James Bama. Could this have been a crossover in the making? The answer was: *NO ...*

came out that later year. Subsequently, I watched the 1966-67 *King Kong Show* Saturday morning cartoon until I knew the theme-song lyrics by heart.

In 1986, as a correspondent for *Starlog* magazine, I stepped onto the soundstage of Dino De Laurentiis's *King Kong Lives* and beheld the great ape lying comatose in a giant surgical amphitheater, awaiting an operation to bring him back to normal functioning after his catastrophic fall from the World Trade Towers at the climax of the 1976 remake. Even reclining, he was an impressive sight.

Out in the back yard of the Wilmington, North Carolina DEG Studios, the rotting carcass of the robot King Kong from the 1976 film sat exposed to the elements, along with other discarded movie memorabilia, such as the giant Green Goblin mask from Steven King's *Maximum Overdrive*.

And so I got to write about King Kong, but as a journalist. But I never imagined writing a King Kong adventure.

I came close when Joe DeVito, who was doing the covers for my *Doc Savage* novels from Bantam Books back in 1992, approached me about writing King Kong's origin. I vividly remember having dinner with Joe in a restaurant at the Empire State Building, appropriately enough, where we talked over our ideas.

I got as far as writing an outline. Ultimately, we went our separate ways over differing creative visions, and Joe wrote *KONG: King of Skull Island* with Brad Strickland, which was released in 2001. That should have been the end of my Kong association. But it wasn't.

The opportunity came around again in 2012 when I called Joe to talk about the 80th anniversary Doc Savage novel that I planned to release in March, 2013. The date was February 28. Joe was again painting the covers to my new series, *The Wild Adventures of Doc Savage*. It was important that this cover be special and have an anniversary theme. Joe reminded me that he was working with the Estate of filmmaker Merian C. Cooper, and suggested a story where Doc Savage meets the Eighth Wonder of the World.

This was an idea fans of both characters had fantasized over for decades. Synchronistically, the Man of Bronze and Kong were linked in the public mind because the first issue of *Doc Savage Magazine* reached newsstands on February 17, 1933, while *King Kong* premiered in New York two weeks later on March 2, going into nationwide release shortly thereafter. Additionally, Doc Savage made his headquarters in the very building from which King Kong made his last stand, the Empire State building.

Consequently, both characters would celebrate their 80th anniversaries within weeks of one another.

Obviously, it was a powerful commercial idea. Yet I hesitated. At that time, I had a limited number of Doc Savages in my contract, and all were planned out in advance. Since most were based on series originator Lester Dent ideas, I didn't want to sacrifice a single one of them.

However, I couldn't walk away from this unexpected opportunity. The first thing I did was ask permission from Doc's owners, Conde Nast, if we could do the project. That response came swiftly.

The fact that approval came on March 2, 2012, the 79th anniversary of King Kong's New York premiere, seemed to be a good omen.

A deal was struck.

Conferring with Joe by phone, together we settled on writing a derivative work based on the 1932 *King Kong* novelization by Edgar Wallace and Delos W. Lovelace. We would not bring King Kong back from the dead. The idea of a Prince Kong was briefly kicked around and discarded.

Inevitably, we realized that a prequel was the only workable approach. This way, Doc and Kong could encounter one another without tripping over the original storyline.

I decided this story would take place after Doc Savage's World War I military service and would involve a journey to Skull Island by ship and the search of Doc Savage's missing grandfather, the legendary sea captain, Stormalong Savage. Part of my inspiration was Merian C. Cooper's 1924 book about his South Seas voyage, *The Sea Gypsy.*

Joe suggested that my novel address Doc's location during King Kong's fatal climb of the Empire State Building, his possible involvement in the climactic battle, and what happened to Kong's dead body after his fall. That inspired my 1933 opening prologue, in which Doc, returning from his Fortress of Solitude, finds Kong's corpse on the sidewalk before his New York headquarters, and stuns his associates when he informs them that "I know this creature." To which the bronze man added, "Long ago, he saved my life. And I returned the favor in kind." We agreed that it was a tremendous start to the kind of epic we envisioned.

After Doc oversees the removal of Kong's massive body to the freighter that will return it to Skull Island for ceremonial burial, the bronze man tells the tale of his encounter with Kong in flashback form.

Because the story was

**Doc Savage,
March 1933**
Art: Walter Baumhoffer

**King Kong,
March 1933**

set in the early 1920s, I realized I could not use the Kenneth Robeson writing style that Lester Dent affected throughout his time on *Doc Savage Magazine*. I went with a modified semi-literary style suggestive of Edgar Rice Burroughs and used my own name instead of the Kenneth Robeson house name.

And so we buckled down to make the book come to life, for, as one of the foremost experts on Kong, Joe would guide me in the development of the storyline, then read and approve the final draft.

Since Joe had evolved his own mythology regarding Kong and Skull Island in *KONG: King of Skull Island,* I was obliged to write it according to his modernized ideas, particularly in regard to the dinosaurs, whom modern science no longer saw as sluggish and brainless behemoths. This included the character of the Storyteller of Skull Island, a native wise woman dubbed Penjaga the Keeper, who had been introduced in *KONG*.

Early in the process, I was pulled out of a sound sleep by visions of sailing ships and the half-familiar word "Nicobar" echoing in my skull. Looking up the latter, I discovered this to be an island on the edge of the Indian Ocean. I took that as a sign that it should be a story locale, and so it became. Otherwise, I have no idea from what subconscious cavern that originated....

Ironically, *Doc Savage: Skull Island* evolved into a sequel of sorts to the book that I was going to write with Joe 20 years before. I took a great deal of inspiration from this, as well as the 1932 novelization of the 1933 film.

Skull Island was released on time for the dual 80th anniversary celebration. Reviews were stellar. Some readers called it one of the best adventure stories they had ever read, and a few considered it the best Doc Savage story they had ever read. I didn't fully believe the latter compliment, but I was quite pleased.

From the beginning, Joe and I were in agreement that we must depict King Kong in a sympathetic and respectful way, in keeping with his status as a global legend. This was not going to be Doc Savage versus King Kong. They encounter one another, but not as enemies. With Joe's blessing, I gave Kong golden eyes to match Doc's so that they would feel a sense of kinship with one another.

For that, we needed a mutual enemy with which these two titans would clash. In researching the native people of the Indian Ocean, I came across the Sea Dyaks of Borneo, who were headhunters. What more fabulous a trophy

Doc Savage: Skull Island **was released in time to mark the 80th anniversary of both characters. Will Murray and Joe DeVito were in agreement to depict Kong in a sympathetic light.**

for headhunters would be than the head of the mighty Kong?

I had my enemy force, and I was ready to start. At its spine, *Skull Island* is the story of the tense relationship between Doc Savage and his father, Clark Savage, Senior, the man who placed him in the hands of various scientists and experts in order to raise him to become a superman, as they ply the Indian Ocean in search of their lost relative.

Once again, I thought that was the end of my professional association with King Kong. But I was wrong.

A year or so after *Skull Island* was published, I acquired the rights to write a new novel featuring on Tarzan of the Apes, the first in decades. This led to a natural and obvious possibility: Tarzan versus King Kong.

Joe encouraged me to write about Tarzan visiting Skull Island, encountering King Kong before his untimely demise. In other words, another lost chapter of Kong's mysterious life. Since Tarzan

was introduced in 1912 and King Kong in 1933, a twenty-year span of time existed during which the immortal ape-man could discover Skull Island before Kong's inevitable and tragic fall.

Once again, I resisted the suggestion. Having written one adventure set on Skull Island, I was not keen on writing another. But I kept the idea in the back of my mind.

The weekend of Edgar Rice Burroughs' 139th birthday came in September, 2014, and my Facebook feed was full of tributes to Tarzan's creator. Something triggered in my mind. My thoughts went back to the idea of Tarzan meeting King Kong. Inspiration struck me that weekend.

During the original 1933 film, the narrative jumps from King Kong being gassed into submission on Skull Island to the eve of his debut on Broadway. We are never shown the ocean voyage during which he was transported.

What happened in between? I wondered. Logically, Kong was loaded onto the tramp freighter that brought Carl Denham's

expedition to Skull Mountain Island — as the mysterious isle was called in the film's 1932 novelization — and so commenced a long and arduous ocean voyage. I knew that Skull Island stood in the misty heart of the Indian Ocean and in between it and New York City — if one sailed westward — lay the continent of Africa.

Perhaps, I mused, there was a story there…

Looking at a map of the Indian Ocean, I realized that the freighter could have gone either west or east in order to reach America. To travel west meant passing through the Suez Canal. But how do you get a gargantuan unconscious ape past a customs inspection?

The same with going east. The ship would have to traverse the entirety of the Pacific Ocean and then, in order to reach New York, steam south and transit the Panama Canal. Customs would hardly approve. Sailing down to the tip of South America was problematic. The Atlantic route was much shorter.

The only solution I

could see would be to circumnavigate Africa. Sailing along the African coast allowed for taking on provisions and fodder with which to feed a shackled Kong, so it was more practical than a Pacific crossing. This would bring King Kong within range of Tarzan's jungle home. It would not be difficult to create a situation in which the ship went aground off the African coast, where King Kong could burst his chains and stomp into Tarzan's personal preserves and create havoc.

That was my jumping off point.

This, I thought, was an idea worth tackling. Here was an untold part of the original *King Kong* storyline. Instead of engineering some excuse for Tarzan to end up on Kong's island and writing a novel in which they played violent tag for any number of chapters, this concept would include the original characters forming the ill-fated expedition to Skull Island, filmmaker Carl Denham, Captain Englehorn and his first mate, Jack Driscoll. And, of course, Ann Darrow.

THE WILD ADVENTURES OF
KING KONG
VS. TARZAN
BY WILL MURRAY

Sailing along the African coast seems more practical than a Pacific crossing — until the *S.S. Wanderer* runs aground and King Kong stomps into Tarzan's territory.   *Art: Joe DeVito*

Rather than Tarzan braving Skull Island, Kong would come to Africa. Africa, a vast continent where he was no longer a monarch, where the wild animals were unfamiliar to him, and where foraging for food would present an unique challenge. Further-more, it was a land where Tarzan had command of all the beasts of the forest.

Here was a work-able concept! Obviously, Tarzan and Kong were ill-matched for a physical confrontation, but backed up by his trusty elephants, his great apes and other animal allies, the Lord of the Jungle could give Kong a worthy battle.

Googling "King Kong versus Tarzan," I was astonished to discover on Wikipedia that Merian C. Cooper had already considered such a project, but was unable to consummate the deal. He couldn't even start planning the production, since RKO Pictures would not release Kong, and MGM held Tarzan firmly in its lion-like paws. The idea was conceived as a prequel to *King Kong*. Well, if it was good enough for the storied creator of King Kong, I reasoned, it ought to be good enough for me.

I telephoned Joe DeVito and explained my idea. Joe loved it. We resolved to reach out to Jim Sullos, President of Edgar Rice Burroughs, Inc., to see if he would agree to such a project.

Happily, Jim did. That very weekend, I sat down and banged out a two-chapter opening, which began with Kong's thrilling capture. It was a perfect start, one designed to set in motion tremendous events.

It took more than a year to work out the deal. In the meantime, I finished my Tarzan novel, *Return to Pal-Ul-Don*. This reacquainted me with the ape man in a way that no amount of novel reading could supply.

During those long months, I thought about how to develop such a story. For a while I was calling the project "Tarzan vs. King Kong," but ultimately realized that this was a King Kong story first and foremost, and Tarzan would be not the primary protagonist, but a powerful human catalyst once the action reached Africa.

Here was a unique storytelling opportunity. Determined and driven Carl Denham serves as the main protagonist. Kong would be the sympathetic antagonist, a tragic figure lost in a strange land, but also the primary menace of the story, control of whom the action constantly revolves.

As for Tarzan of the Apes, he became the heroic protagonist and primary problem solver, whose motivation would be getting Kong out of his jungle before the unstoppable beast-god demolishes it.

Every cast member would have powerful and compelling motivations. There were opportunities for crosscurrents, intrigues, shifting alliances and double-crosses galore.

Here was an epic adventure story, and not just another dinosaur slugfest.

When you begin a novel, whether you outline it or don't, as I rarely do, you imagine it happening more quickly than it does. I thought we would get to the first clash between Tarzan and King Kong by chapter 5 or so. I underestimated what it would take to narrate the capture of King Kong and his loading aboard the freighter, as well as managing him during the voyage to America.

In the original film, King Kong is treated as mythical, a legend among Indian Ocean peoples, until he first appears on Skull Island in all his hirsute glory.

In *King Kong vs. Tarzan*, I reversed that approach. Tarzan is considered myth Africa and doesn't appear until much later in the book, when the situation is so out of hand only the jungle lord's intervention can solve the basic problems.

Imagine my astonishment when, after writing the chapter introducing Tarzan of the Apes, a book arrived in the mail called *Kong: The History of a Movie Icon from Fay Wray to Peter Jackson,* written by Ray Morton. I had ordered it, hoping to learn more about Merian C. Cooper's planned "Tarzan vs. King Kong" project, but the book contained nothing about that mysterious unfilmed movie.

Instead, it revealed to me Cooper's plan for a 1934 sequel entitled *The New Adventures of King Kong.* This project would have followed Kong's arduous transit from Skull Island to New York City, in which the freighter was damaged near the Malay peninsula. During repairs, the ship would be attacked by monstrous creatures from an unknown island. Captain Englehorn would be forced to order Kong released from his chains in order to fight them off. Once this was accomplished, the crew would recapture Kong, and resume their fateful journey.

It turned out my idea wasn't so far off the mark as I had originally thought!

A question arose. Since Tarzan could speak the language of the Great Apes, could he communicate with King Kong? Did Kong even have a language? In the end, I decided to keep it ambiguous. Some of Kong's vocalizations strike Tarzan as familiar, but he is unable to communicate intelligently with the Eighth Wonder.

The reception to *King Kong vs Tarzan* was as gratifying as that of *Skull Island.* I made a great effort to capture the authentic voices of Carl Denham and his crew, and many readers commented that they could hear the voices of the RKO actors in their head as they read along.

From time to time, Joe and I have discussed doing a third King Kong book, picking up where *King Kong vs. Tarzan* left off.

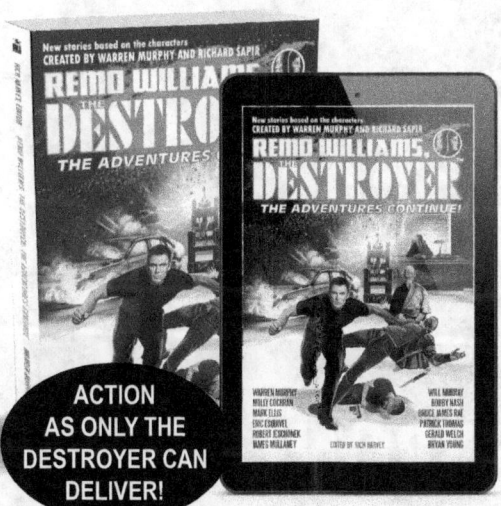

The transit around Africa's Cape of Good Hope to New York City is a long voyage and conceivably other adventures might have transpired during that leg.

I penned a one-page premise. Alas, we've never found time to plunge into that idea. It might seem anti-climatic after *King Kong vs. Tarzan*. But it remains a tantalizing possibility….

Since those books appeared a decade ago, I've gone on to write many more crossovers with classic characters of the early 20th century.

Doc Savage met The Shadow in two novels. Tarzan went to Mars and encountered his fellow Earthman, John Carter, in *Tarzan, Conqueror of Mars* and a sequel, *Tarzan: Back to Mars*. The Spider has teamed up or clashed with numerous of his fellow Popular Publications heroes. Others are in the works.

By sheer luck, good timing, hard effort, and thanks to the confidence of several licensors, I have somehow become the modern king of pulp crossovers.

I owe it all to King Kong! ∎

Will Murray is the author of more than 80 novels, including the Wild Adventures series, which stars *Doc Savage*, *King Kong*, *Tarzan of the Apes*, and other classic characters. As one of the most prolific contributors to *The Destroyer*, he wrote or co-authored more than 40 novels and short stories. His website is adventuresinbronze.com.

LOOKING A LITTLE
HAGGARD

How much influence did H. Rider Haggard's writing have on Merian C. Cooper and King Kong?

by MICAH SWANSON HARRIS

King Kong was Merian C. Cooper's hirsute baby, one he began to conceive in 1929. Four years later, he and RKO Studios delivered his beastly brainchild to movie houses for its first theatrical run.

Of course, ideas come from somewhere, and while Cooper gave the world cinema's first giant "ape," in the early twentieth century there was already an ongoing fascination with gorillas. At the time, they were still a relatively recent discovery by western civilization.

Young Merian Cooper had read the real-life accounts of French-American explorer Paul Du Chaillu who, between 1855 and 1859, was the first to confirm by photographic evidence the existence of gorillas.

Cooper was also a fan of the novels of H. Rider Haggard, the man who created the "lost race" genre with the publication of his first Allan Quatermain African adventure, *King Solomon's Mines*, in 1885. Gorillas and lost races were two tributaries of Cooper's imagination that would one day feed into the mainstream of his story of Kong.

One wonders if the Du Chaillu tributary had already united with the Haggard waters upstream of Cooper. Du Chaillu reported tales of spirits embodying gorillas to abduct native women. This is the basic premise of another of Haggard's Quatermain novels, initially serialized in 1923, *Heu-Heu, or The Monster*.

While Haggard, who had lived in Africa, might have independently heard these stories, it's possible it was Du Chaillu's account that inspired him to pen *Heu-Heu*.

The titular monster is introduced by an ancient

Eexcerpted and adapted from Micah Swanson Harris' forthcoming book on King Kong.

cave drawing depicting an "eleven or twelve feet high…. huge ape to which the biggest gorilla would be but a child, and yet not an ape, but a man, and yet not a man, but a fiend…. (Its) hand grasped by the hair a living naked girl badly drawn…whom apparently it was about to drag away."

In the novel's framing story, speculation has already been raised regarding the survival in Africa of "prehistoric animals or reptiles" after one of Quatermain's friends has cited "an American paper which had stated that a huge reptile of the antediluvian kind had been seen by some hunters in a swamp of the Zambesi…".

Even more on the nose, in one passage Quatermain explains to his faithful sidekick Hans and their Kaffir entourage that "… before there were any men in the world, great creatures…lived there…and, as I had been told, enormous apes much bigger than any gorilla."

So, six years before Cooper began to first think of Kong, is a tale by one of his favorite authors, suggesting the possibility of prehistoric life surviving in remote locations. A more specific parallel is the story's lost civilization's cult of maiden sacrifice, based on the legend of a giant ape.

As Quatermain's adventure unfolds, he learns Heu-Heu's history from an old witchdoctor friend, including how this surviving lost civilization continues to sacrifice "brides" to this approximately twelve-foot-tall ape who lives on an island.

Allan initially dismisses the story as a variant on the myth of Andromeda, but soon he is on yet another of his African adventures to this lost civilization to play Perseus for a contemporary "Andromeda" who the giant ape's cult has lined up for Heu-Heu.

This princess' father

H. Rider Haggard pitted Allan Quatermain against a giant ape in *Heu-Heu* (1924), six years before Merian C. Cooper began developin the idea for *King Kong*.

describes the ceremony in familiar terms, words written ten years before anyone had ever heard of King Kong:

"…(W)e must carry my daughter, on whom the lot has fallen, to the island… and bind her to the pillar upon the Rock of Offering…. There we must leave her, and at the dawn so it is said, Heu-Heu himself seizes her and carries her off…".

Haggard's giant ape is described as "…not an ape, but a man, and yet not a man, but a fiend," language anticipating dialogue in *King Kong* describing *him* as "neither beast nor man. Monstrous…"

For all the build-up, Quatermain and his wingman Hans never buy into the legend and the cult built up around it. Their lack of faith is rewarded when Heu-Heu turns out to be a politically ambitious – and more than a tad randy – high priest on stilts in an ape costume.

Just a few years after *Heu-Heu*'s 1924 publication, Cooper was filming African location scenes for his first Hollywood

movie, *The Four Feathers* (1929). There, he observed baboons' behavior and was struck by how human-like it was, while also hearing rumors of giant gorillas on Africa's west coast.

Perhaps the latter reminded him of Haggard's African-set *Heu-Heu*? I wish that I could say "yea" or "nay." The truth is, I've been reading about *King*

Kong for fifty years, and I've never come across Cooper mentioning this H. Rider Haggard novel in connection with Kong.

His basic plot is well-documented as coming from his friends Douglas and Katherine Burden's expedition to Komodo island and their bringing two of its "dragons" back to civilization. Douglas'

A few years after publication of *Heu-Heu* (1924), Cooper was filming African location scenes for his first Hollywood movie, *The Four Feathers* (1929).

wife Katherine's presence inspired *King Kong*'s beauty and the beast theme.

During this same winter of 1929-1930 that he became acquainted with the Burdens, Cooper saw an airplane passing near the New York Life Insurance Building. From that moment, Kong's climactic iconographic conjunction of prehistoric beast, art deco tower, and modern airpower was set.

While the island cult of maiden sacrifice to Kong was not part of Cooper's original plot, we know how he came to add it to the story.

Haggard's basic plot is well-documented as coming from his friends Douglas and Katherine Burden's expedition to Komodo island. They brought two "dragons" back to civilization.

Concurrent with the development of the *King Kong* script, the native huts for *Bird of Paradise* had been reassembled on RKO's outdoor lot. One night, as Cooper was taking a walk over the lot, he saw a tribal dance number being filmed for the movie.

Watching the choreographed primitive dancing inspired Cooper to think of a lost race sacrificing maidens to Kong in a ceremony similar to what he was watching. This fact would seem to rule out any direct lifting from Haggard of that story element as well.

On the other hand, perhaps this nighttime movie lot encounter triggered memories of Haggard's *Heu-Heu*, and his cult offering up "brides" to what appeared to be a giant ape.

Cooper seems to have had some familiarity, directly or indirectly, with this particular adventure of Allan Quatermain by the early 1930s. To wit:

Heu-Heu climaxes with the "ape's" lake island sinking as the man in the ape costume emerges to claim his latest bride. No worries, y'all. The team of Quatermain and faithful Hans has substituted a veiled corpse for the still very-alive princess (Whew!).

Quatermain uses a well-placed bullet to blow the top off the high priest's ape mask. Soon, this lost race letch is shedding *all* of his Heu-Heu costume before getting carried away by the flood and joining his former island domain at the bottom of the lake.

Anyone familiar with *King Kong*'s sequel *Son of Kong* (1933) will recognize the climactic conjunction of the imagery of giant ape and sinking island, whether you've ever heard of *Heu-Heu* or you Heuvn't.

Given how much the production of *Son of Kong* was rushed to have it in theaters by Christmas 1933 (just nine months after *King Kong*'s debut), I wonder if Cooper, or screenwriter Ruth Rose, borrowed the basic idea of the climax from Haggard's novel to more quickly nail down the script.

It is also worth noting that a dust jacket for Haggard's 1926 *Treasure of the Lake* has art depicting structures resembling the opened colossal doors in the great wall on Skull Island with the sacrificial altar just beyond.

We know H. Rider Haggard was on Cooper's mind during his time at RKO in the 1930s. Just two

Two years after *King Kong* and *Son of Kong*, Merian C. Cooper would adapt H. Rider Haggard's *She* (1935) as producer.

Works referenced for "Looking a Little Haggard"

Behlmer, Rudy. Foreword. *The Girl in the Hairy Paw.* Eds. Ronald Gottesman and Harry Geduld. Avon Books: New York, 1976.

Everett, Eldon K. "H. Rider Haggard: Creator of King Kong?" *The Girl in the Hairy Paw.* Eds. Ronald Gottesman and Harry Geduld. Avon Books: New York, 1976.

Hankin, Mike. *Ray Harryhausen Master of the Majicks. Volume 1: Beginnings and Endings.* Archive Editions LLC: Los Angeles, 2013.

Haver, Ronald. *David O. Selznick's Hollywood.* Alfred A. Knopf: New York, 1980.

Higgins, D.S. Rider Haggard: A Biography. Stein and Day: New York, 1981.

Vaz, Mark Cotta. *Living Dangerously: The Adventures of Merian C. Cooper.* Villard: New York. 2005.

years after *King Kong* and *Son of Kong*, with their hints of Haggard's unacknowledged influence, Cooper would do an outright adaptation of one of the author's most famous novels, *She: A History of Adventure*.

Still, *King Kong* was Merian C. Cooper's concept, and he primarily drew from real life to develop his plot. He had no need to copy H. Rider Haggard's fictional *Heu-Heu*. While there are similarities, the giant ape cult plotlines are by no means point by point.

Given Cooper's familiarity with Haggard, it remains possible that he was reminded of *Heu-Heu* as he developed his idea. The novel might have suggested Kong's description as "neither beast nor man. Monstrous…" echoing Heu-Heu's as "not an ape, but a man, and yet not a man, but a fiend."

Even if unconsciously, *Heu-Heu* could have been the imaginative link between the native dance number for *Bird of Paradise* and Cooper's developing scenario for *King Kong*.

None of the above is plagiarism. Kong is not Heu-Heu. No one owns an idea, only the expression of an idea. *King Kong* was so uniquely expressed as to become instantly iconic. There's a reason "King Kong" is a household name and "Heu-Heu" is not.

Still, there is evidence H. Rider Haggard's Heu-Heu cast a shadow, albiet a small one, on a much larger, and "real," giant ape.   ∎

With Special Thanks to Jess Terrell.

MICHAH HARRIS has previously written about Kong in his article "The Rankin-Bass Kong" in *Wonder* magazine, and in a loose fiction trilogy, *The Eldritch New Adventures of Becky Sharp* (Minor Profit Press), *Ravenwood, the Stepson of Mystery: Return of the Dugpa*, and *Jim Anthony: the Hunters* (with Joshua Reynolds) from Airship27 Publications.

Facts concerning *the* Late Arthur Jermyn and His Family

I.

Life is a hideous thing, and from the background behind what we know of it, peer demoniacal hints of truth make it sometimes a thousandfold more hideous. Science, already oppressive with its shocking revelations, will perhaps be the ultimate exterminator of our human species — if separate species we be — for its reserve of unguessed horrors could never be borne by mortal brains if loosed upon the world.

If we knew what we are, we should do as Sir Arthur Jermyn did; and Arthur Jermyn soaked himself in oil and set fire to his clothing one night. No one placed the charred fragments in an urn or set a memorial to him who had been; for certain papers and a certain boxed object were found, which made men wish to forget.

Some who knew him do not admit that he ever existed.

Arthur Jermyn went out on the moor and burned himself after seeing the boxed object which had come from Africa. It was

By H. P. LOVECRAFT

Originally published in *The Wolverine*, March and June of 1921.

Art: William Heitman

this object, and not his peculiar personal appearance, which made him end his life. Many would have disliked to live if possessed of the peculiar features of Arthur Jermyn, but he had been a poet and scholar and had not minded. Learning was in his blood, for his great-grandfather, Sir Robert Jermyn, had been an anthropologist of note, whilst his great-great-great-grandfather, Sir Wade Jermyn, was one of the earliest explorers of the Congo region, and had written eruditely of its tribes, animals, and supposed antiquities.

Indeed, old Sir Wade had possessed an intellectual zeal amounting almost to a mania; his bizarre conjectures on a prehistoric white Congolese civilization earned him much ridicule when his book, Observations on the Several Parts of Africa, was published. In 1765 this fearless explorer had been placed in a madhouse at Huntingdon.

Madness was in all the Jermyns, and people were glad there were not many of them. The line put forth no branches, and Arthur was the last of it. If he had not been, one cannot say what he would have done when the object came. The Jermyns never seemed to look quite right — something was amiss, though Arthur was the worst, and the old family portraits in Jermyn House showed fine faces enough before Sir Wade's time. Certainly, the madness began with Sir Wade, whose wild stories of Africa were at once the delight and terror of his few friends. It showed in his collection of trophies and specimens, which were not such as a normal man would accumulate and preserve, and appeared strikingly in the Oriental seclusion in which he kept his wife. The latter, he had said, was the daughter of a Portuguese trader whom he had met in Africa; and did not like English ways. She, with an infant son born in Africa, had accompanied him back from the second and longest of his trips and had gone with him on the third and last, never returning.

No one had ever seen her closely, not even the servants; for her disposition had been violent and singular. During her brief stay at Jermyn House she occupied a remote wing, and was waited on by her husband alone. Sir Wade was, indeed, most peculiar in his solicitude for his family; for when he returned to Africa he would permit no one to care for his young son save a loathsome black woman from Guinea. Upon coming back, after the death of Lady Jermyn, he himself assumed complete care of the boy.

But it was the talk of Sir Wade, especially when in his cups, which chiefly led his friends to deem him mad. In a rational age like the eighteenth century, it was unwise for a man of learning to talk about wild sights and strange scenes under a Congo moon; of the gigantic walls and pillars of a forgotten city, crumbling and vine-grown, and of damp, silent, stone steps leading interminably down into the darkness of abysmal treasure-vaults and inconceivable catacombs. Especially was it unwise to rave of the living things that might haunt such a place; of creatures — half of the jungle and half of the impiously aged city — fabulous creatures which even a Pliny might describe with skepticism; things that might have sprung up after the great apes had overrun the dying city with the walls and the pillars, the vaults, and the weird carvings.

Yet after he came home for the last time, Sir Wade would speak of such matters with a shudderingly uncanny zest, mostly after his third glass at the Knight's Head; boasting of what he had found in the jungle and of how he had dwelt among terrible ruins known only to him. And finally, he had spoken of the living things in such a manner that he was taken to the madhouse. He had shown little regret when shut into the barred room at Huntingdon, for his mind moved curiously. Ever since his son had commenced to grow out of infancy he had liked his home less and less, till at last he had seemed to dread it. The Knight's Head had been his headquarters, and when he was confined he expressed some vague gratitude as if for protection. Three years later he died.

Wade Jermyn's son Philip was a highly peculiar person. Despite a strong physical resemblance to his father, his appearance and conduct were in many particulars so coarse that he was universally shunned. Though he did not inherit the madness which was feared by some, he was densely stupid and given to brief periods of uncontrollable violence. In frame, he was small, but intensely powerful, and was of incredible agility.

Twelve years after succeeding to his title, he married the daughter of his gamekeeper, a person said to be of gypsy extraction, but before his son was born joined the navy as a common sailor, completing the general disgust which his habits and mesalliance had begun. After the close of the American war he was heard of as a sailor on a merchantman in the African trade, having a kind of reputation for feats of strength and climbing, but finally disappearing one night as his ship lay off the Congo coast.

In the son of Sir Philip Jermyn, the now-accepted family peculiarity took a strange and fatal turn. Tall and fairly handsome, with a sort of weird Eastern grace despite certain slight oddities of proportion, Robert Jermyn began life as a scholar and investigator. It was he who first studied scientifically the vast collection of relics which his mad grandfather had brought from Africa, and who made the family name as celebrated in ethnology as in exploration.

In 1815, Sir Robert married a daughter of the seventh Viscount Brightholme and was subsequently blessed with three children, the eldest and youngest of whom were never publicly seen on account of deformities in mind and body. Saddened by these family misfortunes, the scientist sought relief in work, and made two long expeditions in the interior of Africa. In 1849 his second son, Nevil, a singularly repellent person who seemed to combine the surliness of Philip Jermyn with the hauteur of the Brightholmes, ran away with a vulgar dancer, but was pardoned upon his return in the following year. He came back to Jermyn House a widower with an infant son, Alfred, who was one day to be the father of Arthur Jermyn.

Friends said that it was this series of griefs which unhinged the mind of Sir Robert Jermyn, yet it was probably merely a bit of African folklore which caused the disaster. The elderly scholar had been collecting legends of the Onga tribes near the field of his grandfather's and his own explorations, hoping in some way to account for Sir Wade's wild tales of a lost city peopled by strange hybrid creatures.

A certain consistency in the strange papers of his ancestor suggested that the madman's imagination might have been stimulated by native myths. On October 19, 1852, the explorer Samuel Seaton called at Jermyn House with a manu-script of notes collected among the Ongas, believing that certain legends of a grey city of white apes ruled by a white god might prove valuable to the ethnologist. In his conversation he probably supplied many additional details; the nature of which will never be known, since a hideous series of tragedies suddenly burst into being.

When Sir Robert Jermyn emerged from his library he left behind the strangled corpse of the explorer, and before he could be restrained, had put an end to all three of his children; the two who were never seen, and the son who had run away. Nevil Jermyn died in the successful defense of his own two-year-old son, who apparently had been included in the old man's madly murderous scheme. Sir Robert himself, after repeated attempts at suicide and a stubborn refusal to utter any articulate sound, died of apoplexy in the second year of his confinement.

Sir Alfred Jermyn was a baronet before his fourth birthday, but his tastes never matched his title. At twenty he had joined a band of music-hall performers, and at thirty-six had deserted his wife and child to travel with an itinerant American circus. His end was very revolting. Among the

animals in the exhibition with which he traveled was a huge bull gorilla of lighter color than the average; a surprisingly tractable beast of much popularity with the performers. With this gorilla Alfred Jermyn was singularly fascinated, and on many occasions the two would eye each other for long periods through the inter-vening bars. Eventually Jermyn asked and obtained permission to train the animal, astonishing audiences and fellow-perform-ers alike with his success.

One morning in Chicago, as the gorilla and Alfred Jermyn were rehearsing an exceedingly clever boxing match, the former delivered a blow of more than usual force, hurting both the body and dignity of the amateur trainer. Of what followed, members of "The Greatest Show on Earth" do not like to speak. They did not expect to hear Sir Alfred Jermyn emit a shrill, inhuman scream, or to see him seize his clumsy antagonist with both hands, dash it to the floor of the cage, and bite fiend-ishly at its hairy throat. The gorilla was off its guard, but not for long, and before anything could be done by the regular trainer the body which had belonged to a baronet was past recognition.

II.

Arthur Jermyn was the son of Sir Alfred Jermyn and a music-hall singer of unknown origin. When the husband and father deserted his family, the mother took the child to Jermyn House; where there was none left to object to her presence. She was not without notions of what a nobleman's dignity should be, and saw to it that her son received the best education which limited money could provide. The family resources were now sadly slender, and Jermyn House had fallen into woeful disrepair, but young Arthur loved the old edifice and all its contents. He was not like any other Jermyn who had ever lived, for he was a poet and a dreamer. Some of the neighboring families who had heard tales of old Sir Wade Jermyn's unseen Portuguese wife declared that her Latin blood must be shewing itself; but most persons merely sneered at his sensitiveness to beauty, attributing it to his music-hall mother, who was socially unrecognised. The poetic delicacy of Arthur Jermyn was the more remarkable because of his uncouth personal appearance. Most of the Jermyns had possessed a subtly odd and repellent cast, but Arthur's case was very striking. It is hard to say just what he resembled, but his expression, his facial angle, and the length of his arms gave a thrill of repulsion to those who met him for the first time.

It was the mind and character of Arthur Jermyn which atoned for his aspect. Gifted and learned, he took highest honors at Oxford and seemed likely to redeem the intellectual fame of his family. Though of poetic rather than scientific temperament, he planned to continue the work of his forefathers in African ethnology and antiquities, utilizing the truly wonderful though strange collection of Sir Wade. With his fanciful mind he thought often of the prehistoric civilization in which the mad explorer had so implicitly believed, and would weave tale after tale about the

Reprinted in *Weird Tales*, April 1924 (above, art by George William Mally) and May 1935 (below, art by Margaret Brundage).

silent jungle city mentioned in the latter's wilder notes and paragraphs. For the nebulous utterances concerning a nameless, unsuspected race of jungle hybrids he had a peculiar feeling of mingled terror and attraction; speculating on the possible basis of such a fancy, and seeking to obtain light among the more recent data gleaned by his great-grandfather and Samuel Seaton amongst the Ongas.

In 1911, after the death of his mother, Sir Arthur Jermyn determined to pursue his investigations to the utmost extent. Selling a portion of his estate to obtain the requisite money, he outfitted an expedition and sailed for the Congo. Arranging with the Belgian authorities for a party of guides, he spent a year in the Onga and Kaliri country, finding data beyond the highest of his expectations. Among the Kaliris was an aged chief called Mwanu, who possessed not only a highly retentive memory, but a singular degree of intelligence and interest in old legends. This ancient confirmed every tale which Jermyn had heard, adding his own account of the stone city and the white apes as it had been told to him.

According to Mwanu, the grey city and the hybrid creatures were no more, having been annihilated by the warlike N'bangus many years ago. This tribe, after destroying most of the edifices and killing the live beings, had carried off the stuffed goddess which had been the object of their quest; the white ape-goddess which the strange beings worshipped, and which was held by Congo tradition to be the form of one who had reigned as a princess among those beings. Just what the white ape-like creatures could have been, Mwanu had no

idea, but he thought they were the builders of the ruined city. Jermyn could form no conjecture, but by close questioning obtained a very picturesque legend of the stuffed goddess.

The ape-princess, it was said, became the consort of a great white god who had come out of the West. For a long time they had reigned over the city together, but when they had a son all three went away. Later the god and the princess had returned, and upon the death of the princess, her divine husband had mummified the body and enshrined it in a vast house of stone, where it was worshipped. Then he had departed alone.

The legend here seemed to present three variants. According to one story nothing further happened save that the stuffed goddess became a symbol of supremacy for whatever tribe might possess it. It was for this reason that the N'bangus carried it off.

A second story told of the god's return and death at the feet of his enshrined wife. A third told of the return of the son, grown to manhood — or apehood or godhood, as the case might be — yet unconscious of his identity. Surely the imaginative blacks had made the most of whatever events might lie behind the extravagant legendry.

Of the reality of the jungle city described by old Sir Wade, Arthur Jermyn had no further doubt; and was hardly astonished when early in 1912 he came upon what was left of it. Its size must have been exaggerated, yet the stones lying about proved that it was no mere negro village. Unfortunately, no carvings could be found, and the small size of the expedition prevented operations toward clearing the one visible passageway that seemed to lead down into the system of vaults which Sir Wade had mentioned. The white apes and the stuffed goddess were discussed with all the native chiefs of the region, but it remained for a European to improve on the data offered by old Mwanu. M. Verhaeren, Belgian agent at a trading-post on the Congo, believed that he could not only locate but obtain the stuffed goddess, of which he had vaguely heard; since the once mighty N'bangus were now the submissive servants of King Albert's government, and with but little persuasion could be induced to part with the gruesome deity they had carried off. When Jermyn sailed for England, therefore, it was with the exultant probability that he would within a few months receive a priceless ethnological relic confirming the wildest of his great-great-great-grandfather's narratives — that is, the wildest which he had ever heard. Countrymen near Jermyn House had perhaps heard wilder tales handed down from ancestors who had listened to Sir Wade around the tables of the Knight's Head.

Arthur Jermyn waited very patiently for the expected box from M. Verhaeren, meanwhile studying with increased diligence the manuscripts left by his mad ancestor. He began to feel closely akin to Sir Wade, and to seek relics of the latter's personal life in England as well as of his African exploits. Oral accounts of the mysterious and secluded wife had been numerous, but no tangible relic of her stay at Jermyn House remained. Jermyn wondered what circumstance had prompted or permitted such an effacement, and decided that the husband's insanity was the prime cause. His great-great-great-grandmother, he recalled, was said to have been the daughter of a Portuguese trader in Africa. No doubt her practical heritage and superficial knowledge of the Dark Continent had caused her to flout Sir Wade's talk of the interior, a thing which such a man would not be likely to forgive. She had died in Africa, perhaps dragged thither by a husband determined to prove what he had told. But as Jermyn indulged in these reflections he could not but smile at their futility, a century and a half after the death of both of his strange progenitors.

In June, 1913, a letter arrived from M. Verhaeren, telling of the finding of the stuffed goddess. It was, the Belgian averred, a most extraordinary object; an object quite beyond the power of a layman to classify. Whether it was human or simian only a scientist could determine, and the process of determination would be greatly hampered by its imperfect condition. Time and the Congo climate are not kind to mummies; especially when their preparation is as amateurish as seemed to be the case here. Around the creature's neck had been found a golden chain bearing an empty locket on which were armorial designs; no doubt some hapless traveler's keepsake, taken by the N'bangus and hung upon the goddess as a charm. In commenting on the contour of the mummy's face, M. Verhaeren suggested a whimsical comparison; or rather, expressed a humorous wonder just how it would strike his correspondent, but was too much interested scientifically to waste many words in levity. The stuffed goddess, he wrote, would arrive duly packed about a month after receipt of the letter.

The boxed object was delivered at Jermyn House on the afternoon of August 3, 1913, being conveyed immediately to the large chamber which housed the collection of African specimens as arranged by Sir Robert and Arthur. What ensued can best be gathered from the tales of servants and from things and papers later examined. Of the various tales that of aged Soames, the family butler, is most ample and coherent.

According to this trustworthy man, Sir Arthur Jermyn dismissed everyone from the room before opening the box, though the instant sound of hammer and chisel showed that he did not delay the operation. Nothing was heard for some time; just how long Soames cannot exactly estimate; but it was certainly less than a quarter of an hour later that the horrible scream, undoubtedly in Jermyn's voice, was heard. Immediately afterward Jermyn emerged from the room, rushing frantically toward the front of the house as if pursued by some hideous enemy. The expression on his face, a face ghastly enough in repose, was beyond description. When near the front door he seemed to think of something, and turned back in his flight, finally disappearing down the stairs to the cellar. The servants were utterly dumbfounded and watched at the head of the stairs, but their master did not return. A smell of oil was all that came up from the regions below. After dark a rattling was heard at the door leading from the cellar into the courtyard; and a stable boy saw

Arthur Jermyn, glistening from head to foot with oil and redolent of that fluid, steal furtively out and vanish on the black moor surrounding the house. Then, in an exaltation of supreme horror, everyone saw the end. A spark appeared on the moor, a flame arose, and a pillar of human fire reached to the heavens. The house of Jermyn no longer existed.

The reason why Arthur Jermyn's charred fragments were not collected and buried lies in what was found afterward, principally the thing in the box. The stuffed goddess was a nauseous sight, withered and eaten away, but it was clearly a mummified white ape of some unknown species, less hairy than any recorded variety, and infinitely nearer mankind — quite shockingly so. Detailed description would be rather unpleasant, but two salient particulars must be told, for they fit in revoltingly with certain notes of Sir Wade Jermyn's African expeditions and with the Congolese legends of the white god and the ape-princess. The two particulars in question are these: the arms on the golden locket about the creature's neck were the Jermyn arms, and the jocose suggestion of M. Verhaeren about a certain resemblance as connected with the shriveled face applied with vivid, ghastly, and unnatural horror to none other than the sensitive Arthur Jermyn, great-great-great-grandson of Sir Wade Jermyn and an unknown wife. Members of the Royal Anthropological Institute burned the thing and threw the locket into a well, and some of them do not admit that Arthur Jermyn ever existed.   ∎

H.P. Lovecraft's work regularly appears in *Pulp Adventures*.

The Happiest Family

A wandering caballero encounters a homesteader with a secret

By RILEY HOGAN

The rider approached a mountain stream. Gently he guided his brown horse to the bank. Rafa lapped at water like a lion gorging on blood.

Diego Aguirre Velazquez dismounted. He was olive-skinned with midnight-dark hair. A cordovan hat overshadowed his hollowed cheeks and strong chin. Spanish-style embroidery distinguished his worn blue jacket. A gun belt rested on his wool California-style pants.

The caballero dipped a rag into frigid water. Diego cleaned his stubbled face with the damp cloth. Gently he wiped grime out of his green eyes.

With clear vision, he stared across the stream at a towering hill. It was taller than a house with a near mercilessly inclined slope. If he crossed the stream here Diego would have to ride up a nearly vertical hill. The slightest mistake could prove fatal.

Diego examined saddlebags full of pelts and furs and retrieved a package from his luggage near the saddle horn. He unwrapped a paste of ground beef and peppers. Rafa stopped drinking to sniff the powerful chili scent. His master ate slowly, paced himself. To finish lunch he sipped from his canteen.

Traveling through the Sangre de Cristo mountains was the best route to Santa Fe. He had been in the highlands for three days now. Better to deal with wolves than lowland desert heat.

Santa Fe was not more than one hundred miles away. There he would sell the furs burdening his horse. The profits would fund his expenses for the rest of the year. There was a time when Diego aspired to buy land and settle down. Now he rarely stayed more than a week in any locale.

Diego's mount stopped drinking at his master's touch. The horse stood erect, like a soldier on guard. Diego climbed into the saddle and gently directed his ally to slowly walk downstream. To find a safer route was vital.

Rafa had served Diego well for three years. The caballero won the horse in a card game against in New Oreleans from Antoine Baristheaut, a mixed Creole who claimed to have been a planter before the war. Diego staked his meager life savings against one of his horses.

Antoine never played without a cigar in hand. Diego noticed the cigar would move up at times; his opponent had a tell! After the third dealing Antoine feigned disappointment but his cigar shifted skyward. Diego folded, ruining the Creole's bet. Even now he could remember Baristheaut agonizing over the horse.

The memories left his mind as he sighted a bend in the stream. Here the hill was much less steep and Diego prodded Rafa into a canter. The beast built up speed as he crashed through low water. Upon reaching the bank Diego lashed at the reins. At the signal his horse galloped towards the hill.

With a sickening jolt Rafa began to run up the slope. Diego slid back in the saddle as his horse thundered uphill. Expertly he shifted his weight forward with both hands gripping the saddle.

Diego was perfectly still as Rafa summited the hill. He knew enough not to push his steed beyond his limits. Especially at times of stress. The horse reached the top in an eruption of energy. Diego lurched sideways as his horse reached the top in a burst of motion.

Pine forest lay before the caballero. He looked over his shoulder to take in a view of the mountains. From the sun's position Diego calculated the time was late noon. Diego slowly rode into the forest. Rafa traced a slow path between sparsely situated trees.

He studied the terrain. His eyes settled on a welcome sight, a column of tracks on the forest floor … a game trail. Diego dismounted. With reins in hand he walked along tracks.

He followed the trail to find a clump of droppings. Instantly he recognized it as deer waste. A wide smile parted his lips. These woods were rich with game.

"Tonight Rafa, *mi amigo*, we feast!" Diego declared to his horse.

"Haaaeeeeeeeeirgg!" A plainly human scream split the silence. A girl. Diego ran in the direction of the cry. He left Rafa behind, there was no time for him to be of use.

"AAAAAHHHHHEIIIIIIII!"

Diego followed the voice into thick brush. He tore through greenery to see a little girl stumbling about a clearing. The child was blonde and appeared to be around six years old. The coyote at the edge of the clearing appeared to be nearly the size of a wolf.

For a second Diego froze in terror. The coyote's white, red coat was stained with mud. It resembled a fox with its extended ears, angular snout. The predator's jaws hung low, exposing butcherous fangs.

Diego drew his pistol. The coyote advanced towards its prey. He opened fire. The sound of the gunshot drowned out the girl's crying as his target collapsed with a bullet near its spine.

Long ears poked into the air. The coyote was only wounded. It sprinted away from the girl, eager to hide in the woods. Diego fired two shots, hitting only air.

Diego charged into the clearing. He stood in front of the girl to shield her with his body. The coyote was paces away from the woods. He took aim at the red and white fur and fired. A faint yelp reached his ears.

Diego left the girl's side to inspect his work. It was vital to kill the coyote to prevent him from coming after her again. Diego reached tangled brush where the coyote lay in pain from gunshot wounds. With one more shot he put the coyote out of its misery.

Diego returned to the child. She appeared healthy without any sign of injury. She had a baby face with a curved birthmark on her cheek. She was barefoot, yet there was not a scratch on her.

"What's your name?"

She thought for a moment. "L-l-lilly."

"Where is your family?"

"Don't know." Lilly slowly explained she had gotten lost while playing.

"Your mama and papa live nearby?" She nodded with blank eyes.

"But you don't know how to get back?"

"Yes," she meekly admitted, shaking her head.

Diego left with Lilly in his arms, following his tracks back to loyal Rafa. With great care he secured himself with the little one in the saddle. Lilly's face beamed with joy with her protector as they rode away.

They returned to the clearing. Diego's keen eyes swept the tree-line. To his left he caught sight of trampled brush. Lilly had left a clear trail. A trail that likely led to her horse.

Diego rode into the forest as Lilly clutched his jacket in an iron grip. It was simple to follow the child's trail of branches and trampled grass. Occasionally he would even find tiny footprints in mud.

Eventually he caught sight of smoke in the near-distance. Somehow he resisted the urge to spur his horse into a gallop for that beautiful smoke. He was eager to return Lilly to her parents. His life was too dangerous for children.

The riders entered a yard dominated by an unusually large house. The two-story home appeared as well built as any army fort and was crowned with a gable roof. Most homesteads were small cabins with one room.

A barn was situated across from the house. An oak tree stood in the center of the yard, halfway between the two buildings.

The caballero climbed down from Rafa. After her ordeal Lilly did not hesitate to jump into his arms. Diego looked up to see a bearded man emerge from the house. The stranger spotted Lilly, broke into a run with open arms.

"Papa!" She called.

"My sweet child."

Father and daughter reunited in a bear hug. Between sobs Lilly told the story of how the brave man saved her from the monster. The bearded man set her down, and approached Diego.

He offered his hand. "I'm Mason Fletcher." Fletcher's midnight dark hair matched his beard.

"Diego Velazquez," Diego said as the two shook hands.

The child's father queried: "You're Mexican?"

"Texian," Diego replied. "My father fought Santa Anna's troops at San Jacinto." His family hated Mexico city rule long before Sam Houston was born.

"Wish I could have been there!" The homesteader's face brightened with admiration, his thought: *This was no foreigner but a fellow American!*

"May I beg a favor? Diego inquired.

"Anything." Mason bent down to pick up Lilly.

"May I use your barn?" He pointed at Rafa.

"Of course!"

Diego left the Fletchers to rejoin Rafa. He led his horse by the reins to the barn. He swung open the door and struggled to see in the dim light.. Hay was piled in the center of the barn. He walked Rafa to a water trough near corner stairs. He removed his luggage and saddle to let his friend rest.

Outside a woman's voice yelled, "Lilly!"

Diego left the barn to see Mason's wife and elder daughter on the porch. Mrs. Fletcher wore her blonde hair in a simple bun. Lilly's sister had brown pigtails. Both wore formal white dresses with flower embroidery.

Lilly and Mason ran to join the other Fletchers. Each took a turn in embracing Lilly. Diego approached the family reunion.

Mason gestured at the blonde woman. "This is my wife Eleanor."

"Just call me Ellie," the beauty chimed in. "Everyone does." Ellie was classically beautiful, blue eyes and high well-formed cheekbones.

"I'm Doris." The brown-haired girl waved. She appeared between ten and twelve years of age.

Ellie picked up her youngest. "You've

already met Lilly."

Mason gestured at his home. "Come inside."

The family herded Diego to the porch. He was ushered into a large common room. Hand carved chairs faced a stone fireplace. The mantle displayed drawings produced by the girls. The floor was littered with toys and cushions.

"Sorry." Eleanor blushed as she picked up items. "We weren't expecting a guest."

"But it's so clean." To Diego's eyes the dwelling was spotless. It had been two months since he had slept indoors. He waited by the doorway, unsure of etiquette.

Ellie returned with a wooden cup. "Here."

"Gracias." He sipped chilled lemonade.

"Tonight dinner is venison," said Ellie. "Please join us."

"I would be honored." Worry crossed his face. "I have to check my supplies."

"You have time, friend. Go on ahead." Mason called from the dining room.

Diego left the house. He sprinted to the barn. He was determined to clean himself up for dinner. The idea of dirtying the Fletcher home sickened him.

He entered the barn to discover a visitor. Little Doris was petting Rafa. The child was startled upon seeing Diego. Gathering up her skirts she broke into a run.

"It's fine, little one," he smiled. "Play with him."

Doris ignored his kind words. She ran past him and out of the barn. Diego followed her into the open. What if the child tripped and hurt herself? His duty as a guest required vigilance.

He watched Doris run to the tree in the middle of the clearing. She disappeared behind the trunk. A smile spread across Diego's face. Doris wanted to play hide and seek!

Slowly he walked to the oak. The child was obviously waiting behind the trunk. Diego peered around the tree to find that Doris was gone. He looked up, expecting to see her perched in branches. Nothing in the oak limbs save for leaves.

Diego hiked towards the house. He was half worried, half stupefied. There was no way she could have left her hiding place without having been seen by Diego. It appeared that the little one had vanished into thin air!

Diego stepped into the common room. Doris was hosting a doll party near the fireplace, but he had not seen her go inside.

"Dinner!" Ellie called.

Doris ran into the dining room. He followed her to find the family at their circular dining table. The table was heavy with venison and boiled potatoes. Mason gestured for Diego to sit across from him. Ellie faced her daughters who shared a bench. After grace Mason gave everyone an equal helping of meat and potatoes.

"We owe you so much," Ellie exclaimed. "You risked your life for Lilly's."

Diego shrugged. "First death then dishonor." It is better to risk death than live with the shame of inaction.

"Where are you from?" Mason asked curiously.

"San Antonio." Diego answered

between bites.

"What do you do for a living?" Ellie asked.

"Trader. But I used to be a vaquero."

"Vuh-kay-ro?" Ellie played with the foreign word.

"A cowman." Vaqueros had taught Anglos how to be cowmen.

Mason spoke up. "Good money in cattle. Why did you leave?"

"If I told you it would upset your daughters."

Silence fell over the table. Diego looked up from his plate to see Lilly. Her cheeks were perfectly smooth. He wondered, *What happened to the child's birthmark?*

Ellie reached for the salt. Diego witnessed a change. For a moment the mother's hand became flat as paper. Time seemed to stop as he stared at a hand.

"Could you pass the butter mister Velazquez?" Mason asked, distracting his guest.

Diego handed over the butter tray. He stared at Ellie … her hand was now normal. *Am I going insane?* Circumstances required him to focus more on remaining calm.

Dinner concluded early in the evening. The men remained seated while the rest went to work. Ellie and her girls packed away leftovers. The remaining food would be pickled or brined.

"Let me help." Diego rose.

Mason forced himself to stand. "Leave the women to their work." He motioned at the door.

Diego followed him out of the house. Mason settled into the rocking chair sta-tioned on his porch. He produced a heavy envelope from his pocket.

"You can stay as long as you like," Mason relaxed. "As long as you sleep in the barn."

"Your barn is a palace," Diego was not lying. To him the barn was paradise after months of sleeping in the open.

"Sorry I can't offer you a rocker, friend." Greedily he ripped open paper containing dark shapes.

"*De nada.* You're welcome." Diego could think of little except Mrs. Fletcher's hand.

"Chew?" He offered the envelope to his guest.

"No." The White man cursed the Indian with alcohol. The Indian used tobacco to curse the White man.

"Suit yourself." He loaded his cheeks with moist wads of tobacco.

Diego explained, "It doesn't agree with my stomach."

"Why did you leave the cattle business?"

Diego silently cursed. He was hoping Mason had forgotten. Thinking quickly, he prepared to lie.

"I joined a cattle drive out of San Antonio." The memory drained his strength. "Some of the finest young *caballeros.*"

"Oh, so you quit because of competition." Mason smiled with inky black teeth.

Diego chuckled before continuing his story. "We camped near the calves." He drew in breath. "My friends woke me at night."

"Woke you?" Mason spat tar.

"We were under attack by … Indians."

Diego almost choked on the lie. "My friends were butchered before my eyes. I barely escaped with my life."

Mason hung his head, meditating on Diego's words. He rocked back and forth.

"You're a survivor, friend." Mason spat tar. "I'm going to tend to the girls. Good night."

"Good night."

Diego abandoned the porch. He hiked into the night. Somehow it didn't seem Mason believed his lie about Indians. He entered the barn and slipped past Rafa. No need to disturb his only friend's rest.

From his saddlebag Diet retrieved a black object. He wanted to read before the sun set. He climbed the corner stairs to reach the loft. Slowly he stretched out on a heap of straw.

Diego opened his bible. It was a Spanish-language edition. He preferred to read scripture in Spanish. It brought back childhood memories of mass in colonial missions.

Scripture helped him with memories of his last cattle drive. Indians did not kill his friends. On the night of the attack Diego chose to camp away from the others. That decision saved his life.

Screams woke him after dark. Diego scrambled up from his bedding. With a torch he ran to help his friends defend against what he believed was a Comanche attack.

Diego reached the main camp to find hell. The attackers were tall, pale gray skin. Giants with teeth and claws like swords. He remembered that the things moved like snakes. One of them looked at Diego with its seven eyes. He saw his good friend Jose butchered like a lamb. A claw like a scythe split his head in two.

The slaughter caused Diego to flee the scene. Like a wild animal he ran for his horse, howls sounding behind him. He rode until sunup. The guilt, shame of leaving his friends would always burden his soul.

In New Braunfels he made a full report to the authorities. The Texas rangers did nothing. The rangers assumed it was a Comanche attack. Diego's report fell on deaf ears, the words of a presumed madman. He learned that Anglos wanted the world to fit into neat little boxes.

Ever since that night Diego had roamed America, searching for answers. Now he was the guest of a family with a secret. Mason's wife and daughters were not human. He would investigate after his reading.

Night came too quickly. The thought of spying on his kindly hosts made him feel filthy. Nothing could stop Diego. Hidden knowledge was one of the few things he lived for.

Diego stole out of the barn. Stealth came naturally to him. His father raised him to silently stalk game through the hills. He advanced towards the candlelight from the house.

Shame inflamed his heart. This generous family had helped him. Now Diego went to repay kindness by skulking around windows. But he walked on, driven by his need to know. Lust for secret knowledge possessed his soul ever since the attack.

Diego came within arm's reach of the house. He approached one window to see into an empty bedroom. Candle light shone in the doorway. Diego circled around the back of the house where he found Doris playing with her sister. Ellie sat in a rocker with a shawl about her shoulders. Normal activity save for one detail. Lilly's hair was red.

Time seemed to stand still as Diego spied on mother and daughters. Eventually Ellie rose from her chair to stand by her children. She stood staring off into space.

Ellie's face … changed. Her face pulsed like a ripple through water. Her skin became clear as glass. Diego looked inside her body to see what looked like smoke with bright lines. Ellie was made of shadows linked by webs of light.

Diego stared in shock at the woman formed from darkness. Slowly his hostess returned to normal. Her face shifted back to healthy flesh.

"Pleasant night, eh friend?"

He turned to see Mason with a pistol. He put a finger to his lip. The homesteader looked more tired than angry. In all his shock Diego had not heard his host's footsteps.

"Senor I was …"

"Walk." Mason gestured a direction with his gun.

The two marched silently around the house. Diego could see within arm's reach. His eyes were adjusting to the dark after spying for so long and was his only chance of survival now. Mason and his hostage approached the doors to a root cellar.

"Open it."

Diego heaved the doors ajar to expose a cavernous hole. Mildew stench filled the air.

"Walk downstairs."

Descending shaky steps, the experience reminded him of when he returned to the massacre site those many years ago … where explored the caves and only found tiny insects. His legs quaked as he reached the floor. The cellar was colder than outside.

For the span of a few heartbeats he stood alone in darkness, then Mason approached. Diego blindly threw himself in the direction of his footprints. By luck he tackled his captor. Two men fell to the ground locked in combat.

Diego struck randomly at whatever he could see of Mason. The battling Texan lashed out with his limbs. He was going to die fighting, not slaughtered like a lamb. Mason ended the fight by stabbing his gun into Diego's ribs.

"I'm not going to kill you." He only planned to use the hand cannon as a prop. "I give you my word."

Mason retreated, allowing Diego to climb to his feet. Light burst out of nowhere, illuminating a room roughly the size of a small cabin. He looked to see the patriarch now held a torch.

By firelight Diego learned he was not in a root cellar. The entire space was a chamber with pillars lining stone walls. A statue stood at the far ended of the room. An idol of a man with a bird's head that approached the ceiling.

"Diablo …" he whispered.

"No," Mason smiled. "The great god Ra of Egypt."

Diego struggled to take everything in. A homesteader with a temple to an ancient god!

Mason declared, "My real name is Caius Julianus Tiberius. I was born Caesar's subject." It was liberating to share his story after so long. He sensed this man, Diego, had been touched by otherworldly influences.

"You expect me to believe that?"

His host shrugged. "Do you believe what you've seen with your own eyes?"

Diego had no reply.

"Ellie, Doris … are part of me."

"*Señor*, everyone's family is a part of each other."

Mason ignored his words. "I spent my youth in Alexandria. I learned from the ancients. I loved Hypatia."

"Who?" Diego nervously eyed the altar. Did Mason intend to sacrifice him to this devil?

Mason sighed in disappointment. "The Egyptians taught me many things." He smiled at memories. "I learned the true nature of the soul."

"*Señor*, anyone who has read the bible knows the nature of the soul."

Mason ignored his words. "The soul has seven parts." *Ba*: personality. *Sah*: spirit. *Ren*: name. *Ka*: vitality. *Ib*: heart. *Shut*: shadow. *Sekhem*: form … each is a separate being."

"*Blasfemia!*" Diego exclaimed.

"I converted to the Egyptian religion." Mason thought back to his initiation. "It was Hypatia who helped me join the mystery cult of Ra."

Diego listened as Mason explained how he rose high in the cult. How he became among the most faithful servants of Ra. Service that was eventually rewarded.

"I learned the greatest secrets about the soul from the arch-priests." Fletcher boasted. "I learned spells to manipulate souls as a surgeon shapes flesh."

The thought chilled Diego to the marrow. He silently prayed for this man to be simply mad.

"It was through my work with the soul that I achieved my greatest triumph. By manipulating my *Sekhem* I became immortal." It was simple to rejuvenate himself with the form part of his own soul.

Diego laughed. "Do it to me and I'll give you a silver dollar."

Mason looked at him the same way any father stares at a stupid child. "I abandoned the cult of Ra to explore the world. But all I found was loneliness. My friends, lovers died off like flies."

Conviction resounded through the man's voice. Diego realized Mason believed every word.

"I once owned the most beautiful slave girl in all of Thrace." Her singing voice was fresh in his mind. "She died of plague after our first month together."

"I'm sorry." Diego felt desperate to keep him talking.

"I found a solution in my studies." His eyes gleamed. "Long ago, I performed a ritual to remove three parts of my soul."

"Your family …" Diego whispered.

"Doris is my heart. Ellie is my vitality. Lilly is my spirit."

"You created ghosts." Now Diego believed every word. Nothing else could explain what he had witnessed.

Mason shook his head. "Not ghosts. The girls have physical forms, they're just not bound by the rules of this world. Rules like space or shape."

Diego felt drunk. After the attack he felt prepared to face the occult. What a fool he had been. His time with the Fletchers made him understand why Anglos pretended the otherworldly did not exist.

"You have my gratitude. My family cannot be harmed but they wander and disappear. Losing them is my greatest fear."

With a shudder Diego realized the reveal was a sorcerer's way of thanking him.

"C'mon friend, let's go back." Mason winked. "Too many spiders down here."

Mason led the way out of the temple and into the open. He left his guest to wander back to the barn.

Diego felt as if he was in a trance. He wandered into the barn, still struggling to comprehend what he had heard. A lonely man had built beauty through unholy rites.

Diego collapsed onto the straw. He saw the Egyptian idol whenever he closed his eyes. Too tired to resist, he drifted off to sleep.

The next morning felt like a dream to Diego. Saddling his horse all went by in a haze. Last night's revelations weighed heavy on his mind. He rode out of the barn to find Mason and Ellie waiting for him. They exchanged farewells.

Diego's horse launched into a canter. What appeared to be children watched him from the windows. He felt Mason's gaze well after leaving the Fletcher homestead.

The *caballero* directed his horse into the pines. Mason achieved happiness. Diego prayed he might one day do the same. First, he had to reach Santa Fe. ∎

Riley Hogan grew up in Texas and Alaska. He is the author of the historical fantasy novel *As Tartary Burns*. He works as a locksmith.

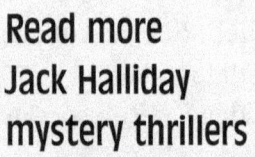

DON'T STIHL CHRISTMAS

Nick Stihl tries to prevent a new name from joining the naughty list

By DR. RICHARD A. OLSON

Christmas, tis the time of the season. An annual festival celebrating the miraculous birth of a baby, not just an ordinary baby; a baby who rocked the world. A baby, Jesus, that changed mankind and the world forever, or so the Catholic nuns told me.

Time to drink, eat, and be merry … or be dead!

Christmas, a time to be merry and bright. A season that's red and green; you could be naughty or nice. It doesn't take a genius to guess which one I am. I'm Nick Stihl, former top ten ranked boxer, now turned Private Investigator. My job is to right the wrongs and punish the wicked all day long. Does that make me naughty or nice?

Children are annoying and pestering their parents, constantly, asking ahead for months, for gifts and presents, and of course for candies, sweets, and peppermints. Adult men looking for mistletoe, an excuse for a kiss, or perhaps an excuse to get slapped. It's the Yuletide season for sure and there are plenty of crooks waiting to score.

With the season, comes Illinois weather. A winter wonderland with ice skaters, tobogganers, and snowballs to throw. And Santa isn't the only one to say *Ho, ho, ho*. Freezing rain, snow, and ice storms galore, these make the prostitutes dress up more.

Snow and more snow, the wiper blade valiantly sweeps back and forth in a semi-circle fighting for driver's visibility and safety. In this weather, I normally play it safe but getting to the office needed to happen. Today is payday for my secretary, Pepper, and she needs to get her check to go Christmas shopping, or so I was told. The windshield of my Packard Eight seems to be losing the battle in the blizzard. The defroster is overwhelmed or maybe it is on holiday and has taken a break. Only seven or eight blocks to get to my office at the Lehman building on Main Street in Peoria, the original Sin City. Leaning forward peering into the windshield and looking through the snowflakes about the size of quarters I can kinda make out the street signs.

I thought of that train trying to make it up the steep hill: I think I can, I think I can, I think I can. Finally, I make it to Main Street, now to find a parking spot. Life is full of challenges. Apparently, going to work today is one of those challenges. I slow down and make a lap around the block watching pedestrians on the sidewalks, hoping for someone to go to their car. The second time around the block, there it is, an early Christmas present. One couple heading to their car, the snow covering the beauty of the Studebaker Dictator coupe. Hitting the brakes and turning on my turn signal, I wait, tapping my fingers on the wood steering wheel. The man opens the door for the woman, she eagerly climbs in, and the door slams shut. The man leans over the hood, brushed off the snow with a gloved hand and enters the Studebaker. A dark-gray puff of smoke exits the tailpipe, my fingers tap the wheel some more and then finally the car motors away into the swirl of white winter wonderland.

Letting out the clutch, there's a slight grinding of the first gear, and I have procured a parking spot. Now the fun part, getting out and going into the Lehman building. I bundle up, wrap the scarf around my trench coat and cinch my fedora over my raven black hair. I push the door open, and a gust of wind pushes back, the result being my shin getting smashed between the door and frame of the Packard Eight. A few unsavory words issue forth from my mouth, but it doesn't matter, nobody hears them. Grimacing, I shove hard, brace the door open and clamber out. My galoshes find stable footing and I more or less close the door, or the galing wind closes it for me. Downtown Peoria is colder than a gold digger's heart and that's cold.

Making my way to the entrance is an exercise in stumbling and slipping on the icy tundra coating the cement sidewalk. Apparently, I'm not the only one having difficulty, a lady nearby slips and stumbles. Reaching out I catch her to stabilize her. The pretty face hiding under the hat and tight blonde curls looked familiar.

"Oh, thank you. It's so nice to see a gentleman nowadays. That would have been a nasty fall for sure."

"No problem, always glad to lend a helping hand." Somehow, I knew those blue eyes from somewhere.

The sparkling blue eyes home in on my steel-grey eyes. "Say — you–you're Nick Stihl."

A smile breaks out on my wind-chapped lips, in spite of the frigid weather. "Wells, Trudy Wells. It seems we keep running into each other."

"Yes, it was at the Pere Marquette, Nick." A couple of snowflakes land on her cheeks, melting into her rouge makeup; another flake lands on an eyelash causing her to blink. Somehow it's a sexy blink and gets my interest aroused.

Being a professional, I ignore my interest and say, "Nice to see you, Trudy."

"Nice to see you too, but Nick I'm disappointed in you. You never visited me at Schipper and Block." Her full ruby-red lips form a pout. Her little pucker is cute; I'd've hated to be her father and ever had to say no to her. "You don't write, you don't call. Do I have to send out smoke signals to get your attention?"

Normally I'm not dense, I saw the signals, but Tudy is a former client. So, I need to tread on thin ice. Thin ice, that's funny with it being winter. There is the ringing of a bell in the background.

"I'm sure something could be arranged, coffee, or a drink perhaps."

Now those wonderful lips went from a frown to a genuine smile. "Now you're talking. A drink would be great, Nick. Preferably something hot."

"Hot does sound good," I say giving her the once over with my eyes.

Trudy is hot-looking indeed. Even in this weather her looks could melt an ice cube at twenty feet. I wonder what kissing her could do. But that drink needs to be later.

I excuse myself, "Unfortunately, I need to get to my office. We could have a drink another time."

Trudy tries to hide a frown. "I understand, we're all busy for the holidays"

Pepper will be unhappy if I'm late, and she is quite the fireball. Her real name is Penelope Boyd, they call her Pepper for a reason.

I want to say something clever, but my ears stop me. Over the sound of the wind, I can hear someone calling out while the bell is ringing. Snowflakes float down on my face, somehow missing the brim of my Fedora. I use my scarf to wipe them off.

Trudy pulls up her jacket sleeve, then her calf-leather gloved thumb pushes down her other glove and looks at her silver Omega lady's watch. "Oh, my God, you're right! I need to get to work also. We are so busy at Schipper and Block with the holidays being here. More than a thousand employees are working there at the moment. It's a madhouse."

Peering over Trudy's wool winter jacket, I see through the white snowy haze the source of the ringing. It's Santa Claus!

"I had no idea they have that many people working." Consoling Trudy I said, "That's a lot of headaches and drama."

"That's right Nick, the other day two of my employees didn't work. One called in sick and another one just plain didn't call."

Consoling her, I want Brownie points. "That does sound tough, you have to do the same amount of work with fewer people."

Trudy nods, "Exactly and there's only so much of me."

I can see Santa ringing a bell, his right hand furiously going up and down like he's trying to shake away the snowy weather. Next to him on a black metal tripod, dangles a red cauldron, well mostly red. It has plenty of snow and ice caked on it. At the top of the tripod, a white sign with a red badge-shaped emblem proudly proclaims the name Salvation Army. Peoria citizens huddling forward fight the weather as they shuffle by and drop change in the slot; occasionally a loose green bill is stuffed in.

I chime in agreeing with Trudy, "That's sure disrespectful not to call in."

When a donation is made Santa belts out ho-ho-ho, and his bell chimes a bit louder and faster.

"Nick you're a sweetheart, thanks for understanding."

I thought maybe she'd kiss me and wondered where the mistletoe was. What I said is, "Not a problem, you're a great gal. I'll help any way I can."

Trudy's face changed expression, "You have helped before, Nick. The blackmail case…" a cloud of pain and sorrow clouds her fine features, "with my deceased husband, Judge Wells."

The whole world needs a hug, so I start with Trudy. She eagerly accepts my hug, perhaps wanting more. Over her shoulder, I see Santa still at work. But someone else is at work also. A young man, maybe a teenager is sneaking up and reaching for the pot of gold — or in this case a cauldron of cash.

Great, crime does not take a holiday. *Hey, that would be a great name for a book or movie.*

During our hug, Trudy starts sobbing on my broad shoulder. The thief's hand touched the metal handle. Santa is occupied talking to two lady shoppers. What's a guy to do? You can't even get a decent hug in this foul stinky world.

It hurt inside but I had to. "Sorry Trudy, there's a job needing to be done." I gave her a not-so-gentle push or more of a shove.

"Nick?!?" She slips and scampers about on her high heels on the icy frozen sidewalk trying to keep her balance.

The welp grabs the bucket and gives a hard yank; the handle comes off the hook. He makes a dash with the cash. Running after someone with totes over my Oxford shoes is not going to win a race.

Santa bellows, his voice rings out, "Stop, thief! Help me, someone help me!"

Apparently now my name is "someone." Well, "someone" was going to help. My right hand reaches for my Smith & Wesson .38 that's tucked comfortably under my suit coat which is under my trench coat. I have shot plenty of guys, wounded some, maimed some, and even taken a few out — forever. But he is just a kid, a punk that deserves another chance. I'm "A Man of Stihl," but I do not have a heart of steel.

Now I remember the joke… What's the difference between a snowman and a snowwoman? Snowballs! In a jiffy I bend over and scoop up snow and pack it together, the heat in my brown calf leather gloves making the snow moist, aiding me. The punk is five yards from me and looks like he was going to be ten yards in a flash.

I put my foot on an imaginary pitcher's mound, take aim like I'm Babe Ruth pitching for the Yankees, and draw back to throw. I wish I had a catcher to call the signals. I nod to an imaginary signal for a fastball. My steel hand whips forward releasing the snowball. It takes off like a rocket after the running youth who is almost ten yards away. The spherical object of snow beans him in the base of his neck, propelling him with his running momentum forward to the frozen tundra of the sidewalk. He hits hard! I can sense or hear his teeth chatter against the hardened cement. He hits so hard he'll have to make an appointment with his dentist.

Trudy cries out, "Great shot, Nick!"

But I barely hear her since I am already rapidly striding and skating over to get the fallen scoundrel. How dare somebody steal from the Salvation Army? A few beleaguered spectators gather around Santa, who has gone to retrieve his mullah. He's gotten to the thief plastered to the sidewalk. Santa with his rotund fake belly is bent over fumbling about, picking up the caldron of cash. The young man attempts to get up, but Santa will have no part of that. He stomps on the fallen thief's back and raises his black-gloved hand with the copper bell and rings the bell.

Ding, ding, ding.

"You will get coal for Christmas!"

Ding!

"Now you will be on the naughty list!"

The bell smashes against the noggin of the young man. His head hits the cement again, like hitting a block of ice. But give the youth credit, he starts to get up again.

Ding!

"No Eggnog for you!"

This time, Santa hit him harder, if that's possible. The bell cracks into two shiny pieces falling to the glittering freshly fallen snow. A low moan emitts from the Christmas robber.

Santa is getting warmed up — in fact ,he's mad as hell. "How dare you try to steal from the Salvation Army? Do want the poor kids to starve?" Santa now starts in on harsher words. Words that even I will not repeat. Words that would make Mrs. Claus blush.

That's where I stepped in, and grabbed Santa's red sleeve, I said one word. "Enough."

Santa trembled and his face was beet red, and it wasn't from the cold. A shrill police whistle sounded out, a "beat cop" was walking over, swinging his Billy club. Looking around it was quite a spectacle, people milling about and next to me was Trudy. She forced a smile showing off her pearly white teeth. The punk started to get up, he had gumption.

Bending over, I yanked him to his feet

by his jacket collar, he was a few inches shorter than me and couldn't have been over eighteen or nineteen. His face was ashen and the look of apprehension on his features told me he was terrified of me. This warning needed to be one time, one time only, so that he would not be a crook or thief the rest of his like. I lifted him up, tightening his collar, so he was standing on his tiptoes, barely breathing.

"Listen up punk!"

He let out a gurgling sound, as I tightened my grip, his eyes were wide and fearful. I pulled back my gloved hand, inside it was a fist of steel. Threatening that I was going to belt him one. My right fist hoover about, like the "Sword of Damocles" was going to strike him down.

In a raspy steel voice, I spit out, *"Don't steal christmas!"*

He fainted and collapsed in my arms.

Trudy gasped. "You didn't you kill him, did you?"

I grimly smiled and shook my head no to Trudy and no for the young man's sake. Hopefully no to the dark path the youth might have taken. No to a life of crime and evil, not on my shift!

Merry Christmas, everyone!

Don't let someone "steal" your holidays.

Dr. Olson grew up training as an athlete, martial artist, and bodybuilder. Today he's a chiropractor, physician, and acupuncturist. He's an avid reader of books, comics and pulp magazines. He is passionate about *film noir* from the 1930's and 1940's. He lives with his wife, two children and a giant white dog on twin lakes outside of Peoria, Illinois.

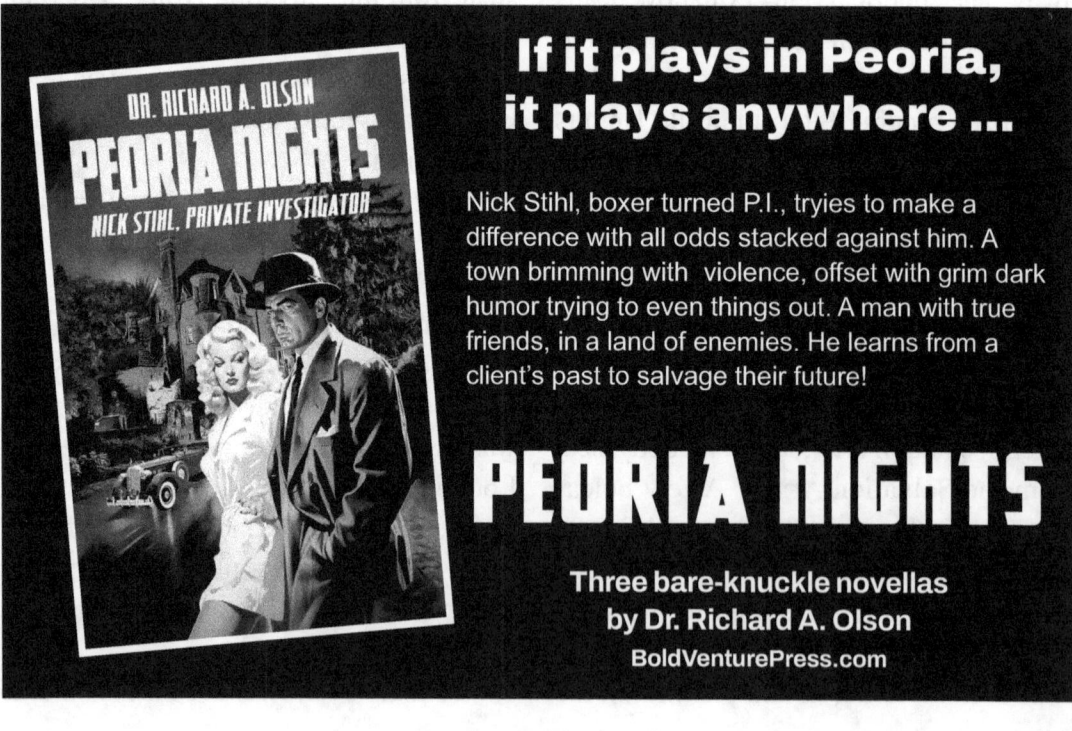

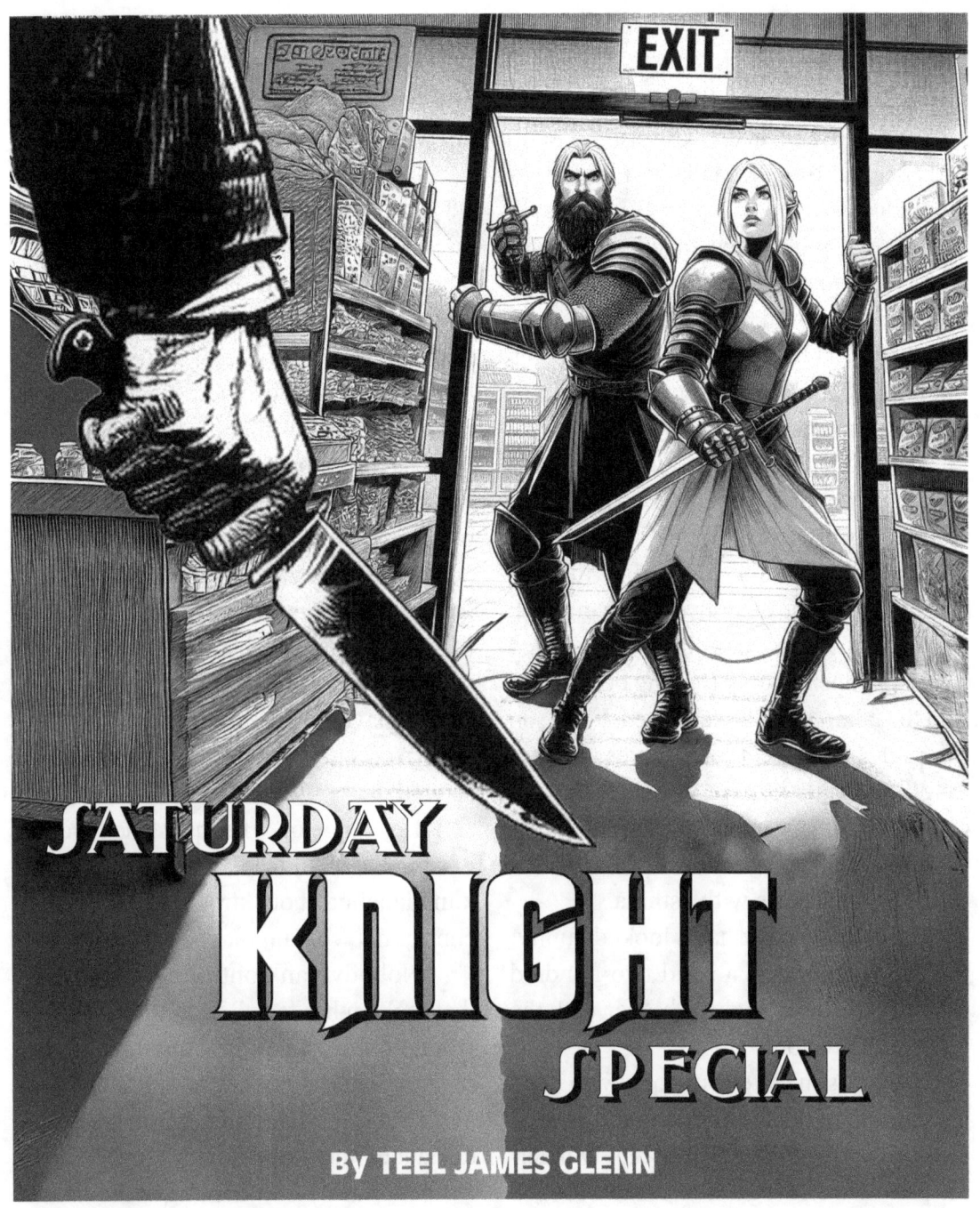

SATURDAY KNIGHT SPECIAL

By TEEL JAMES GLENN

My name is Eric Knight. I'm not a detective, but I play one on T.V as an actor and fight coordinator, which is why I had the old trenchcoat in my closet. And I'm often lazy after filming a show, because my Medieval Faire costume is such a pain to get in and out of, which is why I'd brought the trench

along. I was wearing it over the costume.

I'm also always hungry after a joust, which is why I had walked down through the park to the bodega for some food on the way to the train at the end of the day and I'd had a cheap handgun shoved in my face.

"Hold it right there, mother," some young punk said, waving the cheap gun in my face. He was tall and skinny with a shaven, round head. Combined with bad acne mottling, it made him look truly moonfaced.

Never having been faced with a situation like that before, outside of an old Chester Morris film, I had a dearth of clever ideas. So I fell back on an old reliable one. I hauled off and slapped my female companion Vita across her pretty face.

"Stupid Cow!" I yelled to the shapely blond, "If you didn't insist on condoms we wouldn't be in here!"

The boy with the gun didn't think it was funny, but the other two hoods giggled.

Vita started to tear at the eyes, nodded her head imperceptibly (having beautifully sold the fake slap). She screamed, "You son of a pig!" as she went for my eyes with her long fingernails in pure wench fashion. I caught her wrists and we struggled.

That did it for gunboy who started to laugh like a jackass with asthma.

I guess we must have looked funny; I'm six-foot-six and a solid two-hundred -and-fifty-pounds, looking bigger with the old trench coat on.

She's a slim five-foot-four with long blonde hair, apple-sized breasts, and dressed as a medieval wench, which meant Wonderbra provided cleavage. It must have looked more like she was trying to scale me than fight me. A real crowd-pleaser.

At least it had been when we'd done the same fight for a couple of thousand people earlier that Saturday at the Cloisters Medieval Faire above Fort Tryon Park. It's what I do for a living, stage and perform fake fights. At medieval fairs, in plays, and for movies. Vita was a long-time student

and recent fight partner, though for a bit I'd wished she was more.

Our command performance was in a Korean-owned bodega (only in New York) on two hundredth street and Broadway where we'd walked down through the park to get my tank refueled before hitting the train to our respective homes in Queens.

The three punks had burst into the store and pistol-whipped the old man behind the counter before we knew what had happened. Then they'd begun running through the store grabbing items that caught their fancy and doing their best to terrorize the owner's teenage daughter, Vita, and myself. I don't have much experience with being terrorized either, so I don't think I did it so well.

"Hey, Angelo!" The squat black fireplug of a punk who liked playing with a kitchen knife laughed at our struggles, "If he can't control his woman, maybe we can."

"Nobody can control a woman with that look on her face," Moonfaced Angelo wheezed. He was rooting through the cash register, standing over the injured Korean owner and his daughter, who was trying to staunch the blood on her father's head.

Vita was all but foaming at the mouth, snarling and yelling every invective she knew (some I hadn't even heard before) and apparently trying like blazes to claw my eyes out.

Hidden in the snarls were the Korean words to the daughter. "Stay down and cover him!" We also both studied martial arts with a Korean master, who made us learn the language as well. Hey, I wasn't gonna argue with a seventh-degree. To me Vita added, "Go for Moonface!."

I let her pull a hand free and do the fake eye rake then, her hand swiping across my eyes so fast that no one could see that it was the fingerpads and not the nails that made contact.

I screamed in "pain," called her a "puta" for the benefit of Moonface who laughed harder, and angled myself for what was to come next. My butt was at Moonface, I was doubled over with my knees bent for spring and I was covering my face to hide the fact that there was no blood from the rake.

Vita and I have worked together so long that we practically had telepathy in improvisational acting situations and staged fights. So she could throw her stage right cross close enough to my face that I felt the wind and I could hide the sound effects knap and snap my head around with closeup realism. It rocked me back to within two feet of the counter.

Moonfaced Angelo was laughing and wheezing and trying to yell to us to stop at the same time. "Halto!" He motioned to the third member of the gang with his gun. "Grab her!" he managed to squeeze out.

The third musketeer was a shaven-headed white kid whose face was a map of Ireland. He was a weight lifter and had that monkey man hunch to his shoulders that made you wonder if he had a neck under the bomber jacket.

He made a grab for Vita who slipped him, grabbed bottle of ketchup off the shelf and lobbed it at me.

I dodged.

It sailed past me at shoulder height and almost hit Angelo who flinched and instinctively angled his body to avoid the missile.

That was it.

I stepped on a milk crate that held bags of rice and launched myself over the cluttered counter. I slammed into Moonface's right shoulder, pinning the gun arm to him and slammed both of us into and through the plate glass window of the store.

This was not as nuts as it sounds; I buried my head in his shoulder, kept my hands down behind his body mass, and I had an ace to play: my costume under the trench coat was a chain mail shirt! As I said, I'm lazy after a hard day of pretend fighting and the forty pounds of chainmail is less of a pain suspended from my shoulders and waist (by belt) then balled up in a steel lump in the bottom of my duffle bag with the swords.

So when I hit Angelo I was something like a three-hundred-pound cannon ball that carried Moonface and me a good six feet out onto the sidewalk before I landed on him with a crunch sound from his ribs.

I shoulder rolled off my Hispanic crash-pad, shucked my trench and was back into the bodega door before the glass finished falling from the frame. Vita had blindsided muscles with a second ketchup bottle while he was watching me play Peter Pan. He was sprawled over a potato chip rack, a mass of tomato, hemoglobin, and glass shards.

The Fireplug had Vita backed into one of the aisles with that mean-looking kitchen knife. She didn't dare to try to block and couldn't risk turning to run so she was backing down the aisle flinging cornflake and Bisquick boxes at him.

He was not amused, but bless her

Lithuanian heart, the expression on her face was not fear so much as annoyance.

I didn't relish getting in close to that knife, but I had stupidly left the pistol out on the sidewalk. It might as well have been on Mars because I couldn't leave her alone.

I looked around frantically for something to bean him. My eyes lit on our duffle bag of gear. I ran to it, tore the zipper down, and pulled out my one-handed Viking sword and a round wooden shield.

I faced the aisle and cried at the top of my lungs, *"Odin!"*

Fireplug turned, got one look at me backlit by the streetlight, with my long hair disheveled and with the four-foot blade in my hand, and dropped like a bad lawsuit.

Actually fainted dead away.

After that it was all quick and by the book: 911, paperwork and the inevitable "I'll sue your ass off!" from Fireplug. Muscles and Moonface were still out cold when they loaded them in the ambulance.

One of the cops wanted to book me for possession of a concealed weapon, but his sergeant had done security at the Medieval Faire and saw my day act. The police watched a surveillance tape of the whole affair, so it was safe bet we wouldn't have any legal problems.

It was almost nine o'clock before we climbed on the train. We said nothing the whole trip, just sat adrenaline fatigued and amazed. I tried not to think how sexy and strong Vita looked during the whole thing.

One is not supposed to have thoughts like that about your partner.

But when it came time for Vita to exit at Queensborough Plaza, to transfer to the Number Seven, she didn't budge.

"You're gonna miss your train," I said.

She smiled at me and pulled out a little foil packet I'd theatrically accused her of wanting to get in the bodega.

"You're gonna miss the boat if I *do*."

That Forty pounds of chainmail all but exploded off me back at my place. And I can tell you, once a Knight is never enough!■

Teel James Glenn's novel *A Cowboy in Carpathia: A Bob Howard Adventure* won a 2021 Pulp Factory Award for best novel.

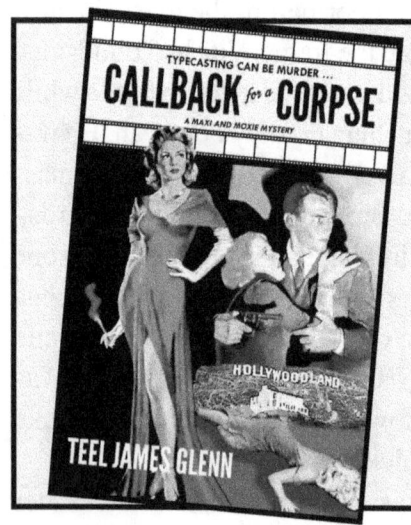

FOOLPROOF

By JOHN RUSSELL FEARN

Judge Rufus Langton sat alone in the library of his small hunting lodge at Railsby Bend. The heavy law book in his hands, the soft cone of light from the desk-lamp, the dark walnut of the shadowed room, were things apart from the raging fury of the winter storm outside.

Only rarely did he glance up. The book was good reading. But he had to keep his eye on the clock. His son and daughter-in-law were due any time, roads permitting

The whining of the wind, the slashing cut of the rain down the long window panes, effectually muffled from him the slight sound of the nearest window catch being lifted with a knife blade. He only became aware of his seclusion being disturbed when the black velvet curtains suddenly billowed inwards and a blast of icy wind surged into the warmth of the room.

Instantly he was on his feet, bewildered, his first thought being that the gale had snapped the window catch. He soon saw how wrong he was as he beheld a figure standing in the opening, a figure in dripping mackintosh and sodden felt hat. An automatic was gripped tightly in his hand.

"Make no moves, Judge Langton! Sit down!"

Langton's legal brain registered the situation instantly. He tightened his lips, dropped into a chair with hands upraised. The intruder reached rearwards, shut the window, then came forward slowly. He stopped when the desk-light glinted somberly on the gun.

"You don't know me, do you? His voice was low-pitched, merciless.

Judge Langton shook his iron-grey head. He was trying to place the lean, rigidly set face, the resolute jaw, the darkly smoldering eyes, the whipcord body.

"No, I don't know you." he muttered, his voice calm. "And I wish you'd come in by the door instead of upsetting me like this. You can put that gun away, too. I am alone, and quite unarmed."

"You think I don't know that?" his visitor asked laconically. "I have kept a tally on your movements for months, Langton — and now you are going to get what's owing to you. Understand?"

Langton's powerful face set into grim lines. He peered again into the shadows.

"Who the devil are you, anyway?"

The man sat down in the chair oppo-site and held his gun steady on the desk edge. "My name's Joseph Gell," he replied slowly. "Does that stir anything in your memory?"

"Gell? Gell?" Langton frowned reflectively, slanted his eyes to the desk drawer containing his own revolver, then shook his head. "I guess it doesn't. I don't seem to — Wait a minute!" he broke off. "Gell! Somebody of that name was condemned to death a couple of years ago. Peter Rayburn Gell. Convicted of murder in the first degree."

The visitor nodded slowly, and raindrops spattered on the blotter from his sodden hat.

"Right!" he acknowledged grimly. "Your memory isn't so bad, at that. Peter Gell was my son. He took the rap because the high-ups responsible for the mess wouldn't come into the open. They left him holding the bag — and you condemned him. Remember?"

"He was convicted of murder," Langton retorted. "Foul murder, Gell. He killed a woman and a man in cold blood. He openly admitted it; and he got the full penalty."

"He died," Gell said slowly, "because he followed orders and wouldn't squeal, a fact which you and that damned jury didn't — or else wouldn't — take into account.

"You guys on the side of justice, so called, have a law that says 'a life for a life.' You might as well know that we fellers on the other side have a law that works out the same way — only sometimes we're a bit longer enforcing it! I say you killed my boy just as if you'd murdered him. You knew the real culprits, but you wouldn't stir yourself to bring them into court!"

Langton smiled frozenly. "Whatever

they did, whoever they were, your son had to answer for his individual crimes! He confessed to murder, and was executed… You're not the first one, by any means, who has tried to get at me for the sentences I've given out—"

"Shut up!" Gell ordered. "You're doing the listening, not me! I vowed when you sent my boy up that I'd get you. Work kept me busy for a time—forging, if you'd like to know. Doesn't that make your hair curl? As soon as I'd cleaned up enough dough, I stepped out and got on your track. I fixed myself at a small place outside this village. I made myself nice and popular with all and sundry — including Sheriff Ingleby. I took the name of Grant and everybody thinks I'm a retired businessman. All so I could be near you. Swell set-up, eh?"

"So *you* are Amos Grant," Langton breathed. "I've heard of you."

"I've waited my chance," Gell went on. "I studied your place here. I figured the best way to get in, the shape of the windows, everything. I knew when you'd be here. I knew even when you'd be alone…" He stopped for a moment and smiled crookedly. "I'm going to kill you, Langton," he said gently.

"And go straight to executioner?" Langton parried, fighting for time. He was in a tight spot and knew it.

"No, not the executioner. This job is foolproof. See?"

Langton's eyes strayed back to his revolver drawer, but Gell's automatic still pointed unwaveringly. Langton forced an apparent calm.

"Gell, you're a damned fool! My son and his wife are coming here later on this evening from Chicago. If you kill me, they'll find my body before you have a chance to—"

"They are, eh?" Gell's eyes gleamed briefly. "Good. Fits in nicely with my plan—"

He broke off as with a sudden lightning movement, Langton's right hand whipped up the heavy law book he'd been reading. In one hurtling movement he flung it unerringly at Gell's hand, spinning the automatic out of his clutch.

Langton dived, snatched at the desk drawer and tore it open. He was too vigorous — the draw came right out and flung its contents across the carpet. Before he could leap Gell had recovered his automatic and stood poised and ready.

"Better take it easy," he advised coolly. "Thanks for doing that. Your own gun will make it simpler…"

He picked it up warily in his handkerchief, jerked it open and glanced at the loaded chambers. He put his own gun away, slipped on a glove, held Langton's revolver steadily.

"Wait a minute—!" Langton shouted hoarsely, but at that identical moment, Gell fired.

The bullet struck clean into Langton's forehead, left a powder mark from the nearness of the fire. A welling trickle of blood went down his ashy, startled face. For a split second he remained standing there motionless — then he dropped heavily to the carpet.

Abruptly Gell was transformed into a man of action. Tearing off his wet hat and mackintosh, he hung them on the fireplace so they dripped to the warm hearth. Then he removed his solitary glove and substituted rubber gloves on both hands, flexed his fingers for a moment.

Working at top speed he commenced a systematic search of the desk, using Langton's own keys. At last he found the material he needed—a bundle of old letters and notes in Langton's own handwriting, together with a fountain pen. To Gell, a man whose very existence depended on his brilliancy as a forger, the next part or the scheme was comparatively simple.

Snatching notepaper he made several scrawls, then began a complete letter. In it he stated briefly that responsibilities, known and unknown, had driven Langton to suicide. The letter was skillfully signed, *'Rufus Langton'*.

Gell read it through, nodded, sealed it in an envelope and penned the superscription — "To Whom It May Concern." He left it conspicuously on the desk.

Then he put the keys back in Langton's pocket, hauled him into the chair by the desk, slumped him in the correct position. The revolver he put on the desk close to the outflung right hand. No slip-ups there, either: Langton had been right-handed all right.

Gell surveyed the result, then looked closely at the carpet for some sign of bloodstain. There was none; he had moved Langton in time… He turned to the fountain pen, but in his urgency to fix it in Langton's fingers, he nearly overlooked the contradictory aspect.

"Can't be," he muttered. "He wouldn't shoot, and *then* write…"

He whipped the pen away, cursed as it fell out of his hand. He turned, looking for it on the floor, trod on it. When he raised it, the nib was cross-legged.

For a moment he was nonplussed. No other pen on the desk: no nibs either, far as he could see. Then his eye caught the glint of a gold clasp on Langton's breast pocket. In an instant he had whipped out a fountain pen and unscrewed the cap. Nib was fairly similar: he could take that chance. He laid it down carefully, suggestively. Not likely this would be a murder problem anyway. He had laid his plan too well for that.

He made a final search, bundled the specimen forgery notes he had made into his pocket, along with the broken pen. The rest was a simple job. He removed all traces of wet from the polished woodwork near the window with his handkerchief, took his nearly dried coat and hat and donned them again, holding up the hems of the mackintosh so no stray drops could sprinkle. Then he retreated backwards out of the room, using the door this time. As he went, he removed all traces of mud he might have left behind.

The front door automatically latched itself behind him as he passed outside.

Immediately the full tearing fury of the wind and rain smote him. Long before he had completed the short journey along the rough shale pathway to his coupe, concealed in the main village road just outside the gates, be was struggling for breath and soddened with the downpour. All to the good, anyway, this weather; wash away all possible signs of footprints.

The moment he had slipped in the driving seat he slammed in the first gear;

soon he was streaking hell for leather down the road. Rain swilled in cascades down the windshield, blurring the vision of half-flooded road ahead. Wind twisted the steering wheel like a live thing in his fingers. He went on at desperate speed, following the only road into Railsby Bend village itself, a distance of perhaps five miles from the Judge's lodge.

The village loomed up at last, sepulchrally dark and gale-swept. Gell's car swished through the puddles of the empty high street, with its dim wavering lamps and rain-glistened houses, lights shining dully behind window shades.

He went on until he came to Sheriff Ingleby's office: then he jammed the brakes and came to a skidding standstill. Leaping from the car he dived for the warm, lighted interior of the place.

Sheriff Ingleby, thin and angular, with a bald head fringed with white fluff, was sitting reading beside the glowing iron stove, pipe in mouth, glasses on nose. He looked up in surprise over his lenses at Gell's sudden wet and spattering entry.

"Why, Mr. Grant! I sure didn't expect to see anybody around here tonight — certainly not you. Anythin' I can do?"

Gell smiled cordially enough under his dripping hat. So far, his plan was working perfectly. Five miles in seven minutes wasn't bad going on such a night. Then his eyes moved from the Sheriff's clock.

"Guess you wouldn't be seeing me now, Sheriff, only I'm nearly out of gas and have another seven miles to cover to get home. The filling station's too far off, even if it's open — which I doubt. I've just come from Chicago, and believe me it's been one lousy trip!"

"Yeah, I can imagine," Ingleby sympathized. He rose stiffly to his feet, and slipped into huge oilskins.

"If I remember right, I've a gallon of gas over in the garage I can let you have. Be right back."

Gell nodded and moved to the warmth of the stove. As he stood there, his mind clarified the last details. The Chicago alibi was foolproof, too: Jed Gunther, big businessman on the surface, racketeer deep down, had promised to provide the necessary verification that Gell had been in Chicago. Of course, a little forging job would he required as payment, but then —

Suddenly Ingleby was back with a can of gasoline in his hand.

"I reckon there's only half a gallon, but you can have it," was his comment. "I guess you—" He glanced round in irritated surprise as the telephone bell sharply interrupted him. Grumbling he moved across to the instrument. "Hope no guy has gotten himself into a mess on a night like this…"

Gell took the can and moved to the doorway. As he stood re-buttoning his mackintosh, Ingleby's words floated to him in snatches —

"Can't get through you say…? Huh? Yeah, sure I understand… Okay, I'll see he gets to know, but I wished you'd picked a better night… What? Sure, I'll do it right now."

Gell waited for no more. He was down the steps, fiddling with his tank, bracing himself against the lashing wind and rain. By the time he had added the spirit to the already half-full tank he was aware that

Sheriff Ingleby was near him, pulling back the doors of his garage.

"Nice dam' job to send a man out on!" he complained, as Gell casually inquired the trouble. "Serves me right for being generous. No need to do it — but I likes to give service…"

"Of course," Gell said, handing over the empty tin and the money.

"Message to deliver — Judge Langton's place," Ingleby growled. "A.good five miles from here, I guess."

He turned away with that, climbed into his own car. Gell hesitated over asking more, then he decided otherwise. The nature of the message did not matter: what *did* matter was that luck was favouring him. Beyond doubt, Ingleby would find the suicide, and the short lapse of time would serve to strengthen the alibi.

Grinning to himself, Gell climbed back into his coupe, started off again into the raging storm.

Fifteen minutes later, Gell was home. His first action was to practically empty the car gas tank in case of a possible investigation, then the legitimacy of his call on the Sheriff could he proved. Oil he also drained plentifully. Generally he left the earmarks of a car that had covered a good distance and consumed plenty of fuel.

Then he went into the house, washed, changed into dry clothes, concealed his automatic, and afterwards repaired to the cosy warmth of his study dining-room to eat a much-needed meal, and reflect on his scheme.

As he ate, the storm, if anything, seemed to increase in fury. The rain beat and splashed against the windows; the wind screamed in every nook and cranny. Momentary thoughts of flood from the River Kilvon, twenty miles distant, assailed his mind. If that happened, he might possibly be washed out by morning. It had happened once: it could happen again.

Then as he considered this unpleasant prospect he was abruptly startled by a hammering on the outer front door. A faint smile touched his hard lips. So Sheriff Ingleby was on a trail of inquiry already, eh? Good!

He opened the door and registered mild astonishment as the dripping form of Ingleby trooped in. He pulled off his oilskins in a flurry of raindrops, then went across to the crackling fire.

"Well, I'm darned glad to be outa that stuff for a few minutes," he declared with feeling. Never saw a night like it in years."

Gell quietly agreed with him, proffered a drink that Ingleby consumed with slow satisfaction. Then he said:

"I'm here to bring a bit of a shock, Mr. Grant. You know Judge Langton, of course? Well, he's — committed suicide."

"No!" Gell's exclamation came in a half whisper of amazed horror: it was just the right inflection. He gave a little puzzled shake of his head. "Well, this is bad news, Sheriff! But — but when did it happen?" he asked curiously. "I was talking to him only two days ago. I suppose it must have been recently, and you found it out tonight?"

Ingleby stood with his back to the fire, shook his head moodily.

"Y'see, I had a message for him: his telephone was out of order with the storm so the message was put through to me. You remember I started off for his place? When I arrived there, there was no answer. I waited a while, knowing he ought to be there somewhere, then as nothing happened, I became worried, and forced a way in. I found him dead at his desk with a suicide confession right in front of him. Shot himself in the head at close range. I left a man down there in charge and went in search of Doc Morgan. He figgered Langton shot himself around eight-thirty tonight."

"Poor old Langton," Gell sighed regretfully.

"Naturally I've to make a few inquiries as to his reasons for suicide. He just said 'responsibilities, known and unknown,' but that conveys nothin'…You say you talked to him two days ago?"

Gell nodded. "I seem to remember he said something about feeling depressed, now I think of it. Tough work, being a Judge."

"Yeah…" Ingleby looked thoughtful. "Did he make any particular statement that might hint at suicide?"

"Not that I recall." Gell was frowning a little now, but still at his ease. What the devil was the old fool getting at, anyway?

Ingleby looked up suddenly from studying the rug. His lean face was grim.

"No, I'm danged sure you don't recall! Langton didn't commit suicide. He was murdered!"

"What!" Gell exclaimed, starting. "But Sheriff, who on earth—"

"Keep right where you are, Grant — if that's your right name." Ingleby's hand was closed now in his right pocket. There was a significant bulge there. "I'm not joking," he added, drawing the revolver to light.

"You're under arrest on suspicion of the murder of Langton."

Gell could not help his gasp of surprise. "Why — you're crazy! What the hell right have you to come in here and make an assertion like that? Why, I was with you at the approximate time of this — this murder! You must remember!"

"I remember," Ingleby said curtly. "But that don't make no difference to me. I'm going to book you! You figgered on a perfect alibi, knowing that it wouldn't be possible to reckon to a few minutes just when Langton died. But you tripped up on one or two things, Grant! You placed a fountain pen in Langton's hand with which he supposedly wrote his suicide confession…

"What happened to the original pen that wrote the note doesn't make much odds: what *does* make odds is the fact that the fountain pen had no ink in it! The barrel was dry as a hone and the rubber tube had a hole in it. Langton musta worn it for an ornament."

The sudden flaw took Gell off his guard. He began to bluster, but Ingleby cut .him short.

"An' there were other things! Scratches on the window-catch, a spot or two of mud from outside, on the carpet, one or two raindrops still slightly wet on the blotting pad…"

Gell flamed, "Damn you, man, flimsy evidence like this isn't going to get you any place! Where's the motive? Anybody might have done it. I couldn't have done it, I tell you! I was driving from Chicago all this evening until I got to your office. Ring up, and find out!"

"I reckon I don't need to do that,"

Ingleby replied grimly. "You say you didn't stop until you got to my place?"

"Right!"

Ingleby seemed to reflect for a moment. "S'pose you know Langton was expecting his son and daughter-in-law tonight, from Chicago?"

"How should I know?" Gell snarled.

"I just thought you might. It was the son who telephoned me at my office — he and his wife are stranded outside Railsby Bend. They wanted me to tell the Judge they couldn't make it."

"So what?" Gell snapped.

"So this! You say you didn't stop any place. What time did you cross the Kilvon River Bridge?"

Gell gestured impatiently. "How should I know exactly? About half an hour before I reached your place, I suppose. Couldn't have been more."

"That's what I reckoned," Ingleby said, smiling bleakly. "A distance of fifteen miles. But the point is that Langton's son also told me that the bridge had been washed away two hours before you got to my place! Yet you didn't stop anywhere! By no possible means could a car have gotten across the river into Railsby Bend tonight! It only struck me later when I remembered you saying you'd come from Chicago."

The Sheriff stopped, his lips taut. "Better get your things. Grant. You've some explaining to do! And hurry up!" ■

John Russell Fearn

British writer John Russell Fearn was born near Manchester, England, in 1908. As a child he devoured the science fiction of Wells and Verne, and was a voracious reader of the *Boys' Story Papers*. He was fascinated by the cinema, and broke into print in 1931, with a series of articles in the *Film Weekly*.

He sold his first novel, *The Intelligence Gigantic* to the American magazine *Amazing Stories*. Over the next 15 years, writing

under several pseudonyms, Fearn became one of the most prolific contributors to the leading American science fiction pulps, including *Astounding Stories*, *Startling Stories*, *Thrilling Wonder Stories* and *Weird Tales*.

During the late 1940s

he diversified into writing novels for the U.K. market, and created his famous superwoman character 'The Golden Amazon' for the prestigious Canadian magazine, the *Toronto Star Weekly*. In the early 1950s in the UK, his 52 novels as by "Vargo Statten" were bestsellers, most notably his novelization of the film *Creature From the Black Lagoon*.

He wrote westerns, romances and detective fiction with equal success.

— *Philip Harbottle*

LEAVE OF ABSENCE

By JOHN BURKE

A number of them rejoiced, in the most decorously sorrowful way, at being rid of Angela. Wonderful, dedicated Angela. Now there would be no more of those lengthy telephone calls denouncing the negligence of the borough surveyor, no more exhortations to join yet another committee to save yet another muddy footpath threatened with extinction, and no more lectures outside the butcher's or greengrocer's on the need for sweeping changes in local government. Poor, relentless Angela. Always so sure she knew what her dear Colin would have wanted if he had lived, and therefore wanting it herself, and therefore insistent that every other right-thinking person must want it.

Now she had gone to join Colin, in the consciousness of having sustained, to the best of her ability, his brave campaigning spirit.

Fletcham parish church was full for the funeral. Resonant phrases of lamentation and heartfelt tribute fell comfortingly from the pulpit. Angela Cardew would be sorely missed. Those gathered here together today could testify to her unsparing work for the whole community. Many heads nodded reverently. A few remained bowed and impassive, among them those of the town clerk and the chairman of the chamber of trade. It would have been in bad taste to let the rest of the congregation see the flicker of a smile, the uncontrollable relief at the knowledge that by-laws, planning permissions, and the litter bins by the shoppers' car park would no longer be subject to Mrs. Cardew's unsparing scrutiny. They wished her well in whatever heavenly mansion had been set aside for her and Colin, in the happy assurance that responsibility for any shortcomings they might find now rested with higher authority.

"One thing you can be sure of," the town clerk had observed to a friend as they entered the cool gloom of the south porch this afternoon: "they'll be having a lot of Extraordinary General Meetings in Heaven these next few months."

Two shocked old ladies scuttled past him towards their regular pews arid settled down to think no ill of the dead.

Jack Paget, sitting beside his wife in a back pew, tried to withhold the absurd prickling of tears in his eyes. For him, too, Angela's departure removed a certain strain. Yet he was sad. It was always sad when an attractive woman died young. At thirty-two, Angela had given off an irresistible physical glow. It offended one — it offended Jack Paget, anyway — to think of such a delectable young widow sleeping alone. Now the glow had been abruptly quenched; but he still couldn't quite believe it, still couldn't accept that he would never again be subjected to the full blaze of those wide grey-green eyes.

Still, at least there was no longer any danger of Angela saying too much to his wife. Knowing her meticulousness, her awful tidiness of mind and morals, he had dreaded the day when "as a matter of principle" — one of her favourite phrases — she would decide that Helen must be told, Jack must explicitly repent, and the whole thing could then be written off.

Not that there was much to tell. Less, he thought ruefully as they stood to sing a hymn, than he would have wished.

It had begun and ended one early evening some ten weeks after Colin was lost at sea.

He and Colin had been friends but hardly close friends. They met at Rotary lunches, at the cold buffet in the town hall on mayoring day, and in the golf club. Jack had flirted with Angela, as many of them did, trying to coax a smile to her pursed but provocative lips and as an unexpected result Helen had started to joke with Angela about it and the two of them came together on shopping expeditions and on a number of committees for saving this, that, or the other.

When Colin was drowned, it was Helen who went to the little fishing village to be with Angela and eventually to bring her home. Angela had taken a lot of persuading. At first she refused to believe that Colin would not reappear. Even when his sailing dinghy was found adrift far out in the Channel, she was sure some passing freighter must have picked him up and would sooner or later radio the news, or that by some miracle he had swam his way to the French coast or the Channel Islands.

"He can't be dead," she said over and over again. "He still had so much to do."

Even when Helen coaxed her back to Fletcham, she could not be still. Several weekends she returned to the coast as if willing Colin to come back into the little harbour from which he had set out — if not the living Colin, then his body so that it might be given worthy burial.

Jack Paget was working late in his office on the Monday after her return from one such vain pilgrimage. He had the details of a property valuation to check, and it crossed his mind that Angela Cardew might soon be putting business his way in the sale of the house which must now surely seem too big for her. There were no children. "Too busy, the two of them, for that sort of thing," someone had once laughed in the bar at the club. "Preservation rather than Procreation — that's their line." Yet looking at her trim but full shape, the way she moved, the sheer quivering intensity of her, you couldn't help wondering…and doubting…and longing…

There was a flush of colour in her usually pale cheeks the evening she came into his office. Perhaps it was a memento of the blustery weekend at the coast.

"An unexpected pleasure." Jack came round his desk and took her hand and made her sit down.

"I saw your car outside. Thought I might catch you."

He perched on the edge of his desk and looked from the sheen of her stocking, tight across her knee, down to the slimness of her ankle. "You can do with a drink." He rolled over the desk and leaned towards the deep bottom drawer. "Don't get the wrong idea. I'm not a secret boozer. Just keep a drop for special clients."

She shook her head, drowsy or despondent — it was hard to tell which — at the quantity of whisky he poured.

"I'm afraid I'm not a very special client," she said in her precise little voice. "In fact, I don't know that I'm going to be a client at all."

Her hair was sleek and short, almost boyish. The whiteness of her neck was only a few inches from his right hand. He made an effort not to reach out and touch it.

He said: "If you want to sell the house and think you'd do better through a London agent, I'll quite understand."

"That's not it at all. I did tell Helen last week I was thinking of selling and finding somewhere smaller, but I don't think I can. I've been worrying on the way back in case you were upset." For once she sounded uncertain, but even as she spoke the resolve was hardening in her mind. "I can't part with it. I owe it to Colin to keep things going." She gulped at her drink and raised her yearning eyes. "I miss him so.

But I know life has to go on."

Jack could no longer refrain from setting his fingers lightly on her warm skin. She didn't flinch, but half abstractedly let her cheek turn towards his hand. Carefully putting his own glass on the blotter, he moved forward so that his arm could slide round her shoulders.

"You've got so much to offer," he said gently. "And so much to enjoy."

"I shall need help. You've all got to help me. Most of all my friends, my real friends."

"You know who you can count on."

Under the fabric of her severely cut black jacket her breasts would be soft and yielding. He stooped further, so that his lips brushed her hair.

"I've got to carry on where Colin left off. They tried to stifle him on the Council. They were scared of the reforms he'd have insisted on. He could have been Mayor of Fletcham. *Ought* to have been Mayor. And just think of how things would have gone if he'd stood as our MP."

Jack tried to think, but was aware only of Angela.

Suddenly she became aware of him, too. She realised what his right hand was attempting. In a split second he was groping for support against the desk while she stood upright and cried: "Do you really think, after Colin, that I'd…that I'd even consider… Jack, haven't you understood a word I've been saying?"

All he had understood were the hypnotic, rhythmic, responsive movements of her body. Too late he realised that they had been responding not to him but to the memory of Colin.

"Can't help it if you have that effect on me," he attempted bluffly.

"It doesn't matter." She sounded unflatteringly as if she meant just that.

He never again saw her with any drink stronger than tomato juice in her hand. When other friends tried to persuade her to have a gin and tonic or even a glass of wine, she would say: "I need a clear head tomorrow." For tomorrow there would always be a meeting. Where once she had stood behind her husband, encouraging him and seconding him and rallying supporters for his innumerable causes, she now took his place. The house was still what it had always been, because she was convinced he would have wanted it to stay that way — a landmark, a lighthouse, something people in the town could turn to in the knowledge that it would show them the right direction in every problem concerning the town, the county, the entire country.

A year after Colin's removal from the scene she pronounced her acceptance of his death by commissioning a memorial plaque for the south aisle of the church. Few dared stay away from the service of dedication.

Now it was Angela's turn. There was a bitter irony in the manner of her going. A minor epidemic of gastro-enteritis broke out in Fletcham, caused by contamination of the old water mains about which first Colin and then Angela had campaigned without result. One old man died, several were in acute pain at home, and a larger number of children had to stay away from school. On her death-bed, Angela almost rejoiced through her agony. Now at last something would have to be done. One could imagine her reunion with Colin, and her triumphant: "We told them so, didn't we? We kept telling them."

Leaving the church to go to the graveside, Jack glanced at Colin's plaque and wondered if Angela had left instructions for the wording on her own tombstone. She would surely not have risked the job being bungled by as much as a misplaced comma.

A week later he was driving past the now empty Cardew house when he noticed Owen Marshall getting out of his car and going up the drive.

Jack parked round the next corner. He had been tactful about the possible marketing of the house when it was a question of the widow's feelings, but now she was gone there was no good reason for being over-delicate with Colin's cousin and family solicitor.

He followed Marshall round the side of the house arid caught up with him on the back lawn, already losing that close-cropped trimness which Angela had imposed on it.

"Ah, Paget." Marshall looked strangely wary.

"Putting the place on the market?"

"Er…" Now the man was positively embarrassed. "Not yet."

"I did hear some talk of Angela having promised to split her money between the Fletcham Heath Conservators and the League for Boundary Reform."

"That's right. In the event of her husband having predeceased her."

"Well, he did that all right."

It was a still morning in the sheltered garden. Yet suddenly there was a swirl like a gust of wind stirring dead leaves into a whirlpool. A voice from far away came swiftly closer.

Angela was coming across the lawn.

She was not visible — not quite, not sharply defined against the dark creeper and the mellow red brick of the garden wall — but you knew she was there, felt her unmistakable presence, and began to hear that unmistakable voice.

"It's dreadful," she was crying. "Dreadful."

Jack Paget knew he was not alone in recognising her. Marshall's face had gone ashen. The two of them backed away and stumbled into a flowerbed. Normally this would have provoked Angela's immediate wrath. But now she was obsessed by one monstrous grievance, more appalling than anything she had ever battled with before.

"He's not there," she raged. "I've looked everywhere…and he's not *there*!"

*****

Angela was back in Fletcham, more active than ever and more insistent than ever. It was worse than it had been when she was still alive: in her new form she appeared to need no sleep, no pause for food, and no time to get from one place to the next.

She kept the vicar awake two nights running, demanding expert opinion on Colin's whereabouts. A shy, gentle, academic man, he aroused nothing but her scorn when he explained that his duties were restricted to this present plane of existence: he welcomed people into the world, solemnised their marriages, preached the truth, did such good works as were within his power, and formally despatched them into the next world. What happened in that next world was beyond his jurisdiction.

"I am sure," he said, longing for sleep as Angela spun and paced and blurred around his bed, "that with patience all will be well. You will find Colin where it is the will of — "

"How can I find him when he's not there? Because I do know he's not there. If he'd been in that place for six months, let alone three years, he'd have had that disgracefully incompetent Records Office tidied up."

When it was obvious that the vicar was too exhausted even to make vaguely soothing responses, Angela turned her attention to some of the clubs and committees she had once belonged to. A number of them owed their existence to her. She had been secretary of one, chairwoman of another, and counsellor to a dozen others. New officers had been elected after her death. They were not too happy when she moved between them on the platform or around the committee table, never settling yet somehow taking over once more all the authority she had been forced to relinquish.

The Fletcham Heath Conservators were the first to suffer. They had organised an evening in her memory, with colour slides of the heath and a talk by a local ornithologist. After ten minutes in the semi-darkness, the small audience of members found that the pictures on the screen were hazing over intermittently, as if a veil were being twitched to and fro. Then, away from the light of the projector, Angela set up a little glow of her own, as though she were a lecturer in a very weak spotlight preparing to explain the scenes they were viewing.

Two women fainted. One rushed for the door and fled. A committee member put the lights on, and Angela seemed to dim a bit; but she was still half visibly, quite audibly there.

"It's disgraceful." She was used to having an audience. There had always been something that needed doing, and something that needed saying, and she had always made them listen to her. They were going to listen now. Her righteous indignation needed an outlet and a response. "Do you realise what a hopeless tangle there is, over there? Quite hopeless. People wandering about in limbo, not knowing how long before they can be moved to better quarters — or downgraded, of course. Impossible to get a straight answer from anyone. And a quite impossible muddle in the book-keeping. Or else why wouldn't they have a record of Colin? I've been in and out of that record office, but they can't be sure of their own files and they don't seem to have any way of contacting higher authority direct."

Too polite to tell her that Colin's been sent somewhere rather nasty, thought one cynic. Spiritual pride and all that. And about time Angela was tipped down there after him.

But nobody would have uttered anything like this aloud. After all, it was generally known that once the estate was tidied up there should be a sizeable legacy coming the way of the Conservators, so it was as well to go on being deferential to Angela for as long as she chose to hang about.

"Remember that trouble we had over the commoners' pasturage and herbage rights, and records of the heathland enclosures?"

There was a slight groan. They remembered.

"How the Council let things drift on and drift on until it was almost impossible to establish the original rulings!" Angela recalled. She flitted agitatedly about the hall. "Over *there,* they've got all the time in the world, or whatever. But can they get their records sorted out? They say" — her astral voice shrilled with outrage — "Colin can't even have got there. It's nonsense, of course. He *must* have got there. They simply bungled his entry documents. But I persuaded them to let me come back, just to make absolutely sure."

"Persuaded them?" said a plump, incredulous woman at the end of a row.

"They said it was quite unorthodox. Wanted me to stay where I was and wait until I was told where I'd eventually be posted. But I wasn't going to hang around. I haven't got time to waste in that sort of bungling. They're so vague that I talked them into letting me make a short return trip."

Even Purgatory, thought the cynic, owed itself a respite from Angela's cross-examinations.

Yet now that she was here, now that she had won her point, she found herself at a loss. It was all very well to lecture her old friends and followers on the iniquities of the after-life: if, over there, they couldn't lead her to Colin, how could anyone on this side do so?

"Just to make sure," cried the wraith with weakening assurance as she went from the Camera Club to the Museum Committee, from the Townswomen's Guild to a dinner party whose guests lost all their appetite for food after a forty-minute harangue.

Colin was not here. She had known that all along. But just to make sure…

"Do you suppose" — it was an inspired suggestion from Helen Paget during a third protracted visit which ruined their television viewing for the third time — "there might be something down at Charhaven? Where you lost Colin in the first place?"

"I went there," lamented Angela, "over and over again."

"Yes, but that was when you were alive. Now that you're… I mean, in these changed circumstances…you might get a different reaction. Some kind of contact."

Angela was ecstatic. Of course. How wonderful of Helen! How wonderful and sensible and how very, very right to see the answer. Because his body had never been washed up, never found, Colin's spirit was still earth-bound — or sea-bound, or whatever you might call it. He still wanted to be found so that he could be decently buried. And he was going to be found now. They would be reunited. Colin's remains would be buried beside her: both on this side and on the other side they would be together.

A spirit herself, she would find it so much easier to seek out his spirit now.

Fletcham was conscious of her leaving for the seaside on a Friday evening; and looked forward to a peaceful weekend. The local sanitary inspector breathed a long sigh of relief. He had all along been anticipating a vengeful haunting until he speeded up work on those lethal water mains. But she had found better things to do.

In Angela's absence, Jack Paget went to see Owen Marshall once more. Helen, pressured by Angela into joining the Fletcham Heath Conservators, had been nominated as Angela's successor on the committee and was now, on behalf of that committee, beginning to ask as circumspectly as possible just when they might expect to receive whatever it was that Angela had left them. There was no secret about her intention to leave them half of what she possessed. Angela herself had let it be known; and Angela, as they all had reason to testify, was meticulous in the fulfilment of promises.

Jack said: "My wife's been wondering — doesn't want to push it, you understand — just how much the Conservators will have to play with when everything's… well, you know, sorted out. And when. Helps the forward planning and that sort of thing, you know."

"Yes," said Marshall.

"No snags?"

"Er…no. The will's straightforward enough."

"So the share-out ought to be made reasonably soon?"

Jack had found in his dealings as an estate agent and valuer that all solicitors were evasive and that no direct question could hope to elicit more than the remotest approximation to a straight answer. But Marshall's expression at the moment was not merely evasive: it was downright shifty.

There was an uneasy silence.

Marshall broke it, clearing his throat. "Angela considered altering her will after Colin's death, but I advised her that it was unnecessary."

"Why?"

"It left everything to her — um — beloved husband. But should he predecease her, then the estate was to be split between — "

"Yes, you've told me that before. And Colin did predecease her. That's it, right — you didn't need to alter the wording?"

"That's right."

But there was something not quite right about Marshall's eager agreement, something that rang a false note.

Suddenly Jack Paget understood. He could hardly credit it, yet he knew it was the only explanation which made sense. He said:

"You persuaded her not to alter the wording."

"Not at all. I explained why, legally, it .was unnecessary — "

"Not only unnecessary, legally," said Jack, "but inadvisable for family reasons. Right?"

"I don't know what you're talking about."

"You do. You're Colin's cousin. You've been taking good care of his property for him until…well, until something happened to Angela."

"He didn't expect it to happen this quickly. There was never any question of…"

Marshall stopped himself. But it was too late.

"Colin is still alive, isn't he?" said Jack. "Where is he?"

"That's ridiculous."

"Come on. Everyone'll have to know, sooner or later."

Owen Marshall groaned. Then he forced a smile, and the creasing of the corners of his mouth foreshadowed a bluff, man-to-man approach.

"All right," said Jack more confidently: "where is he?"

Too late they became aware that Angela was back. She was a seething dust storm in the middle of the room, a fury and a torment and a release of sheer, remorseless energy.

"So that's it," she was crying out of her own private void, "that's it. Where is he?"

*****

Colin Smith, as he now called himself, was coming downstairs from the first-floor sitting room to the shop. He heard the faint chink from the kitchen as Rosemary started the washing-up of their lunch plate at her usual leisurely, unfussy pace. Also he heard scraps of a happy little tune in his head, and began to hum it as he reached the bottom step.

Where Angela met him in a flurry of convoluted nothingness, a storm which did not ruffle a hair on his head yet terrified him in an instant, and said:

"Colin, how could you? How *could* you?"

Behind her — or, rather, through the evanescence of her — was the shop. He had been looking forward to the quiet sat-isfaction of the afternoon there, selling a few batteries and taking in a transistor for

repair, advising on a new cassette player, and explaining to one of the old ladies from the endless city streets why electric light bulbs didn't seem to last as long as they used to. Now the tranquillity of three rewarding years had been shattered.

"I suppose you dug it all out of poor old Owen," he sighed.

"You're not to blame Owen."

"No." He walked on into the shop, visualising the grilling Owen must have undergone. "Wouldn't dream of blaming him. But how did you get back in the first place — and get here? I mean, he notified me that you'd…that there was that nasty business with the drains — "

"The mains."

"Of course. I remember." It seemed so long ago.

From the top of the stairs Rosemary called down: "Darling, who are you talking to?"

Hastily Colin switched on a transistor radio beside the counter which obliged with a news bulletin.

"And who," demanded Angela, "was that?"

"Rosemary."

"And who's Rosemary?"

What was the use of stumbling through evasive explanations? He had often had a discomforting dream in which Angela arrived on the doorstep and he had to confess his deception. Even with flesh-and-blood Angela it would have been tricky. With Angela as am irascible phantom, he didn't stand a chance.

She said: "I want to see this woman."

"No. You can't. It wouldn't… I mean, I…"

There were footsteps on the stairs, and Rosemary came into the shop.

She was a few inches shorter than Angela. Seeing her through Angela's eyes, Colin admitted she was on the plump side, and her smile was too wide and rather naive, and she wouldn't have known how to dress with Angela's crisp, stylish assurance.

But he loved her.

She said: "I'm sure that was you, talking to yourself."

Angela was utterly still, utterly invisible. Colin was acutely conscious of her presence, a few inches away from him. He waited for Rosemary to become aware of this menace, this thing that had come to wreck their idyll.

There was a faint, derisive sniff.

Before Angela could say a word he hurried to the outer door. "Must nip down the road to the post office. Check on those packages that ought to have arrived."

"But Colin — "

"Keep an eye on the shop. Won't be long."

He hurried along the busy pavement with Angela looping round, over, and through other jostling pedestrians, and turned down the first quiet side street, where people would be less likely to notice the muttering movements of his lips.

"Why?" Angela was launched into the inquisition. "Why did you want to sneak out of our life together? For a dowdy little creature like that?"

"You wouldn't understand."

"Colin, you owe it to me to tell me."

"She…we've been…" There were no words.

"You never used to hedge and mumble like this. Whatever has that woman done to you?"

Defiant, he said: "We've been happy."

A man crossing the road looked startled and turned away.

"And weren't you happy with me?" Angela lamented.

It all came out in a rush.

"You expected too much. Of everyone. But most of all of me. There was never any peace, any relaxation. It got too much for me. I'm sorry, Angela, it was cowardly, all right it was cowardly, but I simply had to get out. With Owen's help I shifted a bit of money here and there into an account for Colin Smith — "

"Smith!" she echoed scornfully. "A shopkeeper!"

"I wanted a different sort of life. And you would never have understood. That's why I'm here now," he concluded.

They silently crossed a main road and turned along another back street. He sensed that she was eyeing him up and down, preparing her next onslaught.

"You've let yourself get flabby. Colin, please, before it's too late. Come with me. There's so much that needs doing over there. Really substantial reform. Once you meet the challenge there, I know you'll soon be your old self again. Please, Colin. There's so much for us t do."

He thought of campaigning forever through the perils and frustrations of eternity, a macrocosm of unendingly dissatisfied Fletcham. And he shook his head.

"I'm sure you could choose to come if you wanted to," she urged.

"You mean…kill myself?"

"It wouldn't have to be painful. Once

it was done, we'd be so happy. We'd be together. Working together."

"No," said Colin. "No, I don't see it." Cunningly he went on "They don't approve of suicide, do they? Might send me somewhere quite different. Too much of a risk."

The ghost of Angela went, as it were, wobbly round the edges. He had evidently scored a telling stroke.

He pressed home his advantage.

"I think we have to wait until the proper time. I'll have to come over sooner or later. It won't seem long to you. I mean, the whole time scale must be quite different over there. Now, why don't you just nip back and — "

"I'll wait," said Angela.

"That's my girl. And by the time I get there, I'm sure you'll have learnt a new sort of understanding. You'll see why I did what I did. It'll all be…smoothed out."

"I'll wait," she said, "here."

"But you can't. You have to go back — I don't imagine they'll let you stay on indefinitely? Hm? If they did that sort of thing for everyone — "

"I'm not asking them to do it for everyone. All I know is that they didn't specify any limit to the time *I* could stay."

Colin raised his gaze to the heavens, then lowered it again in case Angela should misinterpret his motives; or, even worse, should interpret them aright. He had a picture of her somehow installed in the room over the shop, accompanying him in his work, disquieting customers and advising him on every aspect of his relationship with Rosemary.

"You can't stay here," he said.

Instinctively his footsteps were turning back towards the shopping centre and his own little, snug little shop.

"Can't I?" said Angela. "You know, I really think you need me. Someone practical. Someone to put you back on your feet again. Someone loyal. Loyal," she repeated so that there should be no doubt about the reproachful echo.

"Go away."

"If you won't be guided by me," she said, I'll find somebody who will."

At the front door of the shop he braced himself, then strode in.

He had been sure Angela would be ahead of him, or beside him. Or close on his heels. But as the bell pinged gently twice, and pinged again, as he closed the door, he knew she had gone. He couldn't believe it.

Rosemary, rearranging four portable tape recorders on a shelf, said: "What on earth have you been up to?" It was a sharper tone than he had ever heard her use before.

He waited for some flickering intimation of Angela's presence. There was nothing.

Maybe she had been recalled. Her time was up.

"Do pull yourself together." Rosemary was even sharper.

"I've been thinking. One or two little legal problems," he improvised.

"Nothing wrong?"

"Not at all, no. You see…well, we didn't expect Angela to die so soon, did we?"

"No."

"I arranged with Owen — at the time I thought there was lots of time — arranged that he should persuade Angela to leave her will as it was. So that when she did die — and we thought that would be thirty years from now, maybe — there'd be something to keep us in our old age. Us: you and me. Just in case we hadn't made a go of things with the shop. But we have made a go of it, and…we certainly don't need that money now, do we?"

Out of a troubled silence Rosemary said reflectively: "Most of it was yours in the first place, wasn't it?"

"Of course. I left it to Angela. You knew that."

"It ought to come back to you."

"But you've never worried about it before. We've never needed it, and we don't need it now. Let the Footpath Fund or the Cats" Home have it."

"There are some larger premises coming up for sale on the other side of the road," said Rosemary. "With fresh capital you could take over, expand the business."

"I don't want to expand. We're happy as we are."

"I think you owe it to yourself," said Rosemary.

Only it was no longer Rosemary. The quietness was Rosemary's, but somehow newly incisive. Only not so new, either. He recognised the tone and went cold. He said:

"Angela, go away."

"I can see you've had a bit of a shock. Do go and lie down for while, and I'll look after the shop. Tomorrow we can talk things over rationally. There's so much to do."

"Angela" — he was desperate — "go away."

"Go upstairs, there's a dear," she said, "and lie down. And you must get Angela right out of your mind."

Right out of my mind, thought Colin with terrible foreknowledge of the months and years ahead. Oh, yes. All very well. But how was he ever going to get Angela out of Rosemary's mind?   ∎

JOHN BURKE

John Frederick Burke (1922-2011) became a prominent science fiction fan in the late 1930s. He was born in Rye, Sussex, but soon moved to Liverpool, where his father was a Chief Inspector of Police.

With David McIlwain he jointly edited one of the earliest British fanzines, *The Satellite*, to which another close friend, Sam Youd was a leading contributor. All three men would become well known SF novelists after the war, writing as Jonathan Burke, Charles Eric Maine and John Christopher respectively.

During the early 1950s he wrote numerous science fiction novels. His short stories appeared in leading UK SF magazines, most notably in *New Worlds* and *Authentic Science Fiction*.

His "Dr. Caspian" trilogy is available from Wildside Press. His crime and detective thrillers are available from Lume Books, whilst his short stories appear in Bold Venture's *Pulp Adventures* magazine.

— *Philip Harbottle*

A THING POSSESSED

By SHELLEY SMITH

Geologists, of course, are accustomed to measure Time in hundreds of thousands, even millions, of years. It seems quite natural to them. But geologists are also human and a mere twenty-five years can seem a considerable span when it is the measure of nearly half one's own individual life, Katherine Pritchett thought wryly. That was how long it was since she had seen London. It struck her the more potently because she hardly recognized it, it had changed so much from the shabby old bomb-shattered city she remembered from 1947.

It was not only that the soot-blackened stone buildings now gleamed airily in the pale pearly atmosphere, it was not only that the once scarred and dingy houses were now trim and bright with fresh paint and there was a stream of brilliant colours ceaselessly moving through the thoroughfares; but the very shape and structure of the place seemed to have altered: roads were no longer where she remembered them, and great glittering boxes stood upended to the sky where once had stood small shops or a row of terraced houses, and here and there a roundabout had swallowed up an elegant Georgian square. It gave Professor Pritchett an odd sensation. In a flash of exceptional fancy it occurred to her that that might be how ghosts felt when they returned to earth, except that Professor Pritchett had no such irrational superstitions.

She had some difficulty locating the block of flats where the Duchemins lived and feared she would be late. She should have taken a taxi, it had been foolish of her to walk, but the day was so fine, so spring-like…

Professor Duchemin had taught Political Economy at Toronto University at the same period as herself. That they were both English created a bond, and he and his wife had been very kind to her. Then the Duchemins had returned to England and she had gone soon after to Berkeley University in California. They continued to write to one another, at least at Christmas. And when Katharine came back to London she phoned them and they had at once asked her to lunch.

Millie kissed her.

"We want to hear all about everything. Come and sit down."

"You know what happened to Winterton at McGill, don't you?" said Harold, beginning to laugh.

"Now don't swamp her, Harold. Let her get her breath. She's so pale. Why are you so pale, dear?"

"Am I?" said Katherine, smiling. "I'm perfectly well."

"You don't look it."

"It's nothing." She laughed. "I had a fright just now—in Leinster Gardens."

"Why?"

"I don't know. I've no idea."

"But one can't be frightened without a cause, can one?" Millie observed reasonably.

"Evidently one can, Millie. It was just a wave of irrational terror, and now it's passed."

"Well, if you say so, dear. Not a sherry. Harold, I'm sure Katherine would rather have a brandy."

"Sherry's fine," Katherine protested.

"It's no good arguing with Millie, surely you remember that. If Millie says you'd rather have a brandy that is what you must have."

"You're very kind."

"Men never notice anything," said Millie, confiding a feminine glance at the other woman. She watched her swallow a little of the brandy. "Why Leinster Gardens, I wonder? Did you live there once?"

"No, never." She began quickly to ask Harold if the book was nearly finished, and presently Millie pottered off to the kitchen to chivvy the pans around, leaving the professors to their interminable gossip about shop.

Later, Professor Pritchett wondered why she had lied to Mrs Duchemin. She was essentially a truthful person, not in the habit of lying to get herself out of an uncomfortable corner.

In the literal sense it was true enough, she had never *lived* in Leinster Gardens, but—

It was so long ago, nearly half her lifetime. So deeply was the recollection buried in the lumber-room of memory that Professor Pritchett remembered nothing about it until Millie Duchemin had started probing into the wherefore of that spasm of unreasoning fear which had shaken her as she passed through Leinster Gardens. And then it was no more than a thin edge of memory like a light shining through a crack at the foot of a door. On leaving the Duchemins she went back there to look for the house.

She hardly remembered what the house was like, except that it was a big Victorian terrace-house the yellowish-brown colour of old ivory, with steps running up to a heavy pillared porch. There had been a black-printed notice in the front window saying room to let, which had caught her eye.

It was extremely fatiguing tramping the streets to find a room that was both clean and quiet and not too depressing. This one had a broad turkey-carpeted staircase leading up to it, and the good solid furniture reminded Katherine comfortingly of her grandmother's house in Manchester. Perhaps it was because of that and because it was near the park that Katherine decided it would do.

"Two pounds ten a week, payable in advance," she remembered the landlady saying in a soft Scottish voice. "Use of bath extra."

Katherine must have been twenty-eight or -nine at the time; old, like a good many other people then, to start a career. But the war had caught her in the middle of her studies. There was just time to sit for her degree before she was called up. When she was demobbed she took a six-month refresher-course and then spent a year in fieldwork. After that there seemed to be nothing for her to do and she came to London to try and get a post as a lecturer, with any luck somewhere abroad in a country that had not been devastated by war.

Katherine collected her cases from the station, managed to get them on to a bus and then lugged them down the street and up the stairs to her room where she unpacked them, shook out each garment fastidiously and hung them in the immense satinwood wardrobe with the mirror which sent back a sallow unflattering reflection of her face. She saw in its dim recesses something dark move behind her. Or she had the impression that she saw something, but when she turned quickly nothing was there, nothing dark like a vase or a clock on a bracket which might by an optical illusion have appeared to move. Katherine concluded that some dark bird must have flashed past the window at that moment or perhaps the curtain had swayed in a draught.

London was a dismal city in 1947. Katherine found a cafe in the High Street that was at least warm and bright, where she ordered one of those death-defying meals to which people had become accustomed. She chose a Vienna steak, which had absolutely no connection either with

Vienna or steak; it was sliced tinned meat fried in batter; but at least it was less repulsive than disguised whale meat or an unappetising fish called snoek. If it was not actually nourishing, it filled the stomach.

A more real and satisfying nourishment was the concert Katherine went to afterwards at the Albert Hall; an extravagance she did not regret, for she returned to her lodgings feeling less despondent than she had for some time.

It was raining a fine drizzle and her coat was quite damp when she took it off. Too damp, she thought, to put in the wardrobe. She hung it from the pediment of the wardrobe. But twice it fell down, slightly startling her each time as she lay reading a paperback edition of *A Passage to India,* and she was obliged to get out of bed to hook it back again. The third time she gave in and hung it in the wardrobe and firmly closed the door.

She read for only a little while and then put out the light and sank into a deep and dreamless sleep. She was awakened some time later by an angry rattling noise. In that moment between waking and sleeping it sounded to her like thunder distantly reverberating. Then she realized it was the wind shaking the window in its frame. Damn, she thought, I'll have to find something to wedge it with; I'll never be able to sleep with it like that. She uttered a petulant sigh and switched on the light. The noise ceased. All was quiet. But of course it couldn't have been the wind, there was no wind that night.

She waited a little, and then turned off the light once more and lay down. Presently she dropped back into sleep.

The sound pierced her slumber like someone shaking her shoulder to awaken her. She started up. In the dark, to her sleep-fuddled senses, the rattling pane was like sinister laughter. She turned on the lamp again and at once all was as quiet as before. If it was not the wind then it must be caused by the vibration of passing traffic, one of those particularly massive lorries trundling their lonely way through the night hours perhaps.

Katherine flung back the bedclothes and went over to the window. The top of the lower frame was well above her eye-level, but she groped with her fingers for the catch. She had thought it might not be properly 'fastened, but it was. In fact it was so tightly fastened that for all her efforts she could not release it. The window had evidently not been opened for years and the catch was stiff with rust and grime. She banged the frame lightly with her fists to try and find out where the loose bit was, but it didn't budge. Oh well, she would mention it to Mrs Macrae in the morning.

Now her hands were filthy. Katherine lifted the ewer and poured a little cold water into the basin. She was winding her hands round the soap when a flash of light from the wardrobe-mirror behind her caught the corner of her eye as the door swung open. Out of the dark interior a shapeless brown object flew towards Katherine. She eyed it dumbstruck with terror and incomprehension. It seemed to be continuously changing its form as it advanced. It flopped to the carpet just before it reached her and lay in a crumpled heap. Almost before she had realized that it was her skirt, Katherine saw her fawn jumper whirl from the dark depths in the same way. And then another garment. And another.

Katherine stood there, her hands slippery with soap, her head twisted over her shoulder, staring at the extraordinary phenomenon. It was exactly as if these things were being hurled at her malevolently by someone *inside* the wardrobe who was in a terrible rage. It had the effect of making Katherine feel terrified. A shoe hit her on the shoulder. She *was* being attacked.

Katherine half turned away and shook her hands quickly in the cold water. The wardrobe was empty now. She picked up the basin and turned to empty it into the slop-pail, when she saw the turned-back sheet on the bed rise up — as though somebody was using it to masquerade as a ghost.

Katherine never could remember afterwards how she managed to get out of that room. She spent the rest of the night huddled at the top of the stairs, listening...

When morning came at last, she went back to pack her things. The room seemed ordinary enough by daylight. Katherine might have believed the entire episode to be the figment of a nightmare if it had not been for the disorder. Firming her will, she picked up the clothing and crushed the garments hurriedly into the cases. When she was dressed she went downstairs and found Mrs Macrae.

"I'm sorry, I've changed my mind. I can't stay here."

Mrs Macrae looked at her without speaking. Then she said slowly: "The room wasn't comfortable?"

"It doesn't suit me."

"Then you must have your money back," said Mrs Macrae and fetched her purse. She counted out forty-three shillings and slid the money delicately towards Miss Pritchett, who met the landlady's eye with a long considering glance and then picked the money up.

"Thank you."

"No, I have to thank *you*," said Mrs Macrae in a low voice. "Not everyone is as nice about it."

Katherine stared.

"You mean you know?" She said angrily: "But you have no right to let the room in those circumstances."

"It's my livelihood, miss. What would you do?"

"I wouldn't let unsuspecting people sleep there, I know that. It could kill anyone with a weak heart, or frighten a person out of their wits," she said indignantly.

"I know. You're right of course. I do try to exercise judgement about whom I let it to. And she doesn't always— Well, She doesn't object to everyone, it seems."

"She? You know it's a she? You have seen something, someone ...?"

"No. I haven't seen Her. But I know who it is," Mrs Macrae said, turning away. The kettle spluttered on the stove. "Miss, you'll do me the favour of taking a cup of tea before you go; I can't let you leave like this."

Katherine hesitated, longing only to be gone from the place, but the look of appeal in Mrs Macrae's sad violet eyes held her back. She pulled out a chair and sat down at the kitchen table.

A grateful smile eased the landlady's strained face. She set out a place for her and whisked from beneath the grill the rasher of bacon and piece of fried bread she had been keeping warm for her own breakfast and laid it in front of Miss Pritchett. "It's little enough to do," she said firmly when the young woman protested.

"But it's your ration. I can't take it."

"I don't need it, and it would please me better to see you eat it," she said in her precise Scottish way. She set the brown earthenware teapot on the table and seated herself behind it. Gazing down into her cup, the landlady said on a note of quiet desperation: "There is no one to whom I can talk about it."

"If I were you I think I should take some advice from those who know about such things. Why not consult the Society for Psychical Research? I'm sure they would help."

"I don't think I could do that. I mean, once it got out that the place was haunted no one would ever come here again. And then what would I live on?"

"Yes, I see. But you can hardly let things go on as they are either, can you?" Katherine hesitated. "I'm not religious myself, but I rather think that if I were in your shoes I should be tempted to try anything. Have you thought of asking some ecclesiastic to exorcize the room? That is often effective, they say."

"I appreciate your kindly intentions, miss, and I'm afraid you will think me very 'difficult' and stupid, but," Mrs Macrae turned her head aside, "I couldn't bring myself to do that to her even now. You see," she said, drawing her finger round the contour of a dull stain on the cloth, "who knows what *happens* to a ghost who is exorcized? We only know they are banished. But where to?" she murmured, leaving nameless questions in the air.

Katherine was chilled. Perhaps the woman was a little bit mad. Katherine really looked at her for the first time. She was quite old, fiftyish, with abundant dark hair turning grey. She must have been pretty once; she had still a certain pathetic charm. No, she was not mad: just honourable.

Katherine said: "You speak as though you knew her."

Mrs Macrae nodded.

"Oh yes, I knew her, more's the pity. She was my husband's mother. She hated me from the first. She never wanted Dick to marry me. And when he died, she held me to blame. So now she revenges herself. She has tied me to the house till the day I die, because she knew there was no other way I could earn my living."

"Could you not sell it and perhaps buy a small business with the proceeds?"

"Under the terms of the will I am not allowed to sell, or even let it; I am obliged to live in it, and may not even will it away. When I die it will go to a Cats' Home." Mrs Macrae gave a faint laugh.

Katherine looked shocked. "I've never heard of anything so venomous. The will ought to be contested."

"Oh no, my dear. There's nothing to contest, even if there'd been the money to take it to court. A mother-in-law is under no obligation to provide for her son's widow. Some people might think I was lucky, and

I suppose I am. Only," her voice trembled, "I sometimes wonder how much longer I can bear it." She smiled shakily. "Let me give you another cup, my dear. It's done me so much good to talk to you."

"I'm afraid I've not been of much help," murmured Katherine who did not believe in ghosts, though it seemed rude to say so to someone who believed herself to be haunted. Moreover, it was impossible to deny that she had been badly frightened by something. Now in broad daylight, she began almost to doubt the validity of her own fears. "This — this thing that you say you've never seen: how do you know it's the ghost of your mother-in-law?"

"Why, who else would it be, dear? This is her house and that was her room. And if you had known her as I did, you would recognize her unmistakably by the way she behaves. She was always a violent and self-willed person."

"But what would be the purpose behind this unreasoning malice?"

"Who can tell! Perhaps she doesn't even know herself. Perhaps she is no more than a blind mindless force. Perhaps that's what being a ghost is, like a record needle stuck in a groove, playing the same notes on and on, until maybe someone releases it."

Miss Pritchett never saw Mrs Macrae again. But about six months later she was shocked to see in the paper that a Mrs Macrae had been murdered in her home in Leinster Gardens. She went out at once and bought all the newspapers she could find.

Piecing the information together as best she could, she learned that the woman had been discovered lying in her night-clothes on a bed in an upper room, her body enveloped in a sheet with which it appeared she had been strangled. Several items of silver were missing from a cabinet. The police were anxious to contact a man believed to have stayed at the house on the night of the murder. None of the papers mentioned in which room the murder had taken place.

A week later she read that a man was said to be helping the police with their inquiries. And forty-eight hours after that it was reported that a thirty-two year-old man, name of Ronald James, had been arrested for the murder of Mrs Janet Macrae on the night of the eighteenth of that month.

Why shouldn't the man have murdered her? Katherine thought, and tried to put the matter from her mind. But it kept creeping in and taking her unawares. If only she knew which room it had happened in, but she hadn't the least idea how she could go about finding out, for she was in Nottingham at the time. And anyway there was nothing she could do, was there? If the man was innocent he would be released. If he was guilty then it was better she should not interfere. It really was none of her business.

Ronald James was committed for trial at the Old Bailey. A force stronger than her own judgement took Katherine to London, the college having broken up for the long vacation.

The house in Leinster Gardens was closed up, and something about its desolate appearance brought the reality of the situation home to her as nothing else had. It was no longer just a newspaper story: it was true. Seeing her staring up at it from the other side of the road, a woman paused beside her and with a residue of communicativeness left over from the war announced: "You can't see the room from this side, it was at the back. I mean, if that's your interest in the house."

"I knew Mrs Macrae."

"Oh? Poor soul! A terrible thing to happen to anyone, whatever they may have done. But I always say it's asking for trouble for a woman alone to let rooms to single men. Still, being a widow she would have been lonely. I'm not blaming her," said the woman quickly, "it's not for us to judge one another, is it? I know what it's like, having lost mine."

Katherine said stiffly:

"I don't know what you're talking about."

"Don't mind me. It's none of my business, after all. But you can't get away from the fact that she was in her nightie when they found her, dead, in the man's bed on the second floor back. It speaks for itself, doesn't it?"

There was no need for Katherine to listen to any more, once she had learned that the murder had taken place in the 'second-floor back'. It meant she *had* to do something. She went to the police and said she had some information for the Defence in the case of Rex *v* James, and could they put her in touch with the accused's solicitor.

"Miss Pritchett?" said Mr Ableman, the solicitor, a smooth, middle-aged, balding gentleman, rising from behind his desk to greet her. "Do sit down. I understand you have some information for us concerning our client, Ronald James."

"I believe he is innocent."

"So do we," said Mr Ableman suavely.

But she knew that he didn't mean it. This smooth gentleman would never believe anyone to be innocent. And suddenly Katherine felt herself to be old-maidish, ridiculous, provincial—seeing herself through his sophisticated superior eyes. She pulled off her gloves and loosened her coat.

"It is a difficult story to tell," she began. "But I want you to listen to what happened to me in that room on the second floor back a few months ago."

Mr Ableman put his fingertips together and listened quite patiently. She had feared he would laugh. But he didn't. When she had finished, he was silent for a moment or two, and then he said:

"It was good of you to come, Miss Pritchett. It can't have been easy. And you mustn't think I doubt the veracity of your story. I am sure it happened exactly as you say. But you are an intelligent woman, you must see that one could not put it forward as a feasible defence. It would simply be laughed out of court. It assumes too much. It is asking rather a lot of anyone to believe that an intangible ghost—always supposing there really are such things—could have the physical strength to strangle anyone."

"It requires power, not physique. It was the *sheet* that strangled her, don't you see."

"I'm sorry,' said Mr Ableman, shaking his head."

"You're not going to do anything about it then? Even though it may mean an innocent man will be hanged."

"I have great faith in British Justice," said Mr Ableman, bowing.

Katherine was in court on the first day of Ronald James's trial. She listened to the Prosecution's counsel outlining the case against the prisoner to the ladies and gentlemen of the jury. It was through the pieces of silver he alleged he had bought from the murdered woman that he had been traced. He alleged that he had paid Mrs Macrae twenty-five pounds for the teapot, milk jug and silver salver; but the money was never found. (And so on and so forth.)

Ronald James sat in the dock, looking as unperturbed as though all this had nothing to do with him. He was a handsome little man, with a jaunty, sensual, conceited expression. If looks were anything to go by he might well be guilty.

At any rate, they hanged him.

Professor Pritchett stared up at the vast office building standing where once the Victorian houses had been. She was glad the house was no longer there. The ghost must have departed with it: ghosts can hardly haunt modern offices, there could be nothing for them to do in those bleak functional edifices. The sheer unreasoning terror which had struck her earlier as she passed through must have only been the long-forgotten memory rising unbidden from some deep recess in her mind.

Mustn't it?   ∎

SHELLY SMITH

"Shelley Smith" was the pseudonym of English writer Nancy Hermione Bodington (1912-1998), used for her writing following her marriage to Stephen Bodington in 1933. She was the author of 15 highly-regarded detective and psychological crime thrillers, published between 1942 and 1978. Her earliest short stories (of which "Crooked Harvest"is one) were published by Gerald G. Swan, who published her first novel *Background to Murder.*

An Afternoon to Kill (1953) is regarded by critics as her best novel. Also notable was *The Ballad of the Running Man* (1961) which was successfully filmed by Carol Reed as *The Running Man* (1963) starring Laurence Harvey and Lee Remick. She was also a co-writer of the film *Tiger Bay* (1959). All her novels are currently in print from Lume Books in the UK.

— *Philip Harbottle*

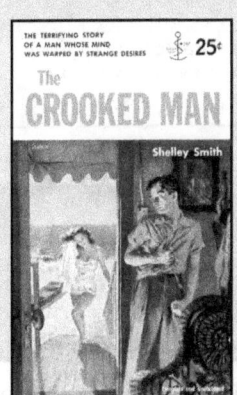

ROUGH EDGES

(Continued from page 88)

lone film sale, serving as the basis for the Wild Bill Elliott vehicle *Hands Across The Rockies*, as detailed by Bill Pronzini in his introduction and Ed Hulse in his afterword.

"Their Guardian From Hell" (*Star Western*, March 1937) is a hardboiled tale featuring a self-loathing gunman who protects a family of settlers from the villains out to steal their land. In "Leetown's One-Man Army" (*Star Western*, October 1941), a drifter named California Tracy with a score of his own to settle finds himself in the middle of a war between a cattle baron and some sodbusters, a traditional plot that Davis enlivens with some fine writing and a nice twist.

The title story, "Dead Man's Brand", is from the November 1942 issue of *Star Western*. In it, drifting cowboy Dave Tully tries to claim an inheritance and finds himself framed for a murder: his own.

"The Gunsmoke Banker Rides In" (*Star Western*, July 1942) is another well-plotted Western mystery about a banker who's surprisingly fast with a pair of .41 caliber derringers.

This volume also includes three stories from earlier in Davis's career. "Death Creeps" (*Action Stories*, December 1935) finds troubleshooter Dave Silver being hired to find the Creeper, a mysterious murderer who kills from the darkness.

In "Sign of the Sidewinder" (*Western Aces*, June 1935), Tom Band, an American cowboy framed for a murder he didn't commit, is broken out of a Mexican prison to carry out a mission of vengeance for his benefactor. This is my favorite story in the collection, a great noir adventure yarn. Tom Band returns in the almost as good "Boot-Hill Bait" (*Western Aces*, November 1935), which finds him on the trail of a fortune in outlaw loot. If there are any more Tom Band stories, I'd love to read them.

Davis's smooth prose is a joy to read, and he handles humor, emotional torment, and lightning-paced action all with equal ease and effectiveness. These are simply some of the best-written Western tales you'll ever read, and *Dead Man's Brand* is a great collection. It gets my highest recommendation.

WHEN THE DEVIL CAME TO ENDLESS, Charles Boeckman

I'm a big fan of Charles Boeckman's Western pulp stories, but *When the Devil Came to Endless* is the first Western novel of his I've read. Published by Avalon in 1996, it came out long after the pulp era was over, but it shows that Boeckman had lost none of his top-notch storytelling ability.

WHEN THE DEVIL CAME TO ENDLESS

by Charles Boeckman
AN AVALON WESTERN

Endless is a small town in West Texas, and as the book opens, a huge, deadly tornado is bearing down on it. The twister strikes with incredible force, devastating the town, leaving death and destruction in its wake.

Boeckman spends the first half of the book using flashbacks to give us the stories of several people affected by the tornado: the young man convicted of a murder he didn't commit; the preacher's daughter who's in love with him; the preacher facing the greatest test of his faith he's ever known; the scheming banker; the firebrand newspaper editor, and several other citizens of Endless. Boeckman skillfully makes all of these into well-rounded characters instead of the stereotypes they might have been. They all have plenty of problems before the tornado strikes, but things are going to get worse, because just as the town is starting to clean up after the storm, a mysterious stranger rides in and brings even more danger...

When the Devil Came to Endless is a really well-paced book that kept me turning the pages all the way to its very satisfying conclusion. In addition to being a fine traditional Western novel, it's also a fairly clued murder mystery, and Boeckman

handles both elements well. The setting also rings true, as anyone who's spent some time in West Texas will know. It's excellent work from a top professional and gets a high recommendation from me.

DOOM PLATOON
Richard Gallegher
(Len Levinson)

Readers of the World War II series *The Sergeant* by Gordon Davis may notice some similarities between those books and the novel *Doom Platoon* by Richard Gallagher. *The Sergeant* features a big, ugly, extremely tough non-com, Sergeant Mahoney. *Doom Platoon* features a big, ugly, extremely tough non-com, Sergeant Mazursky. Graphic violence abounds in both (although to be fair, these are war

novels). There's plenty of crude, politically incorrect dark humor. None of these similarities come as any surprise when you realize that Gordon Davis and Richard Gallagher are actually the same person: veteran paperbacker Len Levinson.

Doom Platoon came out a couple of years before *The Sergeant* began. You could regard it as a sort of dry run for the later series. But it can certainly be read with enjoyment on its own. During the Battle of the Bulge, the platoon of the title is under the command of Sergeant Mazursky after their lieutenant is killed in action. These 29 men are posted on a ridge above a narrow road, and their mission is to stop an entire Panzer division from advancing and hold the road until the retreating American army can regroup. It's a suicide mission, of course, and the first half of this novel is very intense as Mazursky and his platoon try to fight off the overwhelming Nazi forces.

Then, halfway through, *Doom Platoon* becomes a P.O.W. novel as the survivors from the battle are taken to a German prison camp, and the rest of the book chronicles what happens to them from then until the end of the war. While this part of the book doesn't have the urgency of the first half, it's still very well done and keeps the reader flipping the pages.

It's kind of a reviewer's cliché to say that prose is compulsively readable, but Levinson really does have that knack. His characters may not be particularly likable, but he makes you want to find out what's going to happen to them. This book, originally an obscure paperback from Belmont-Tower, is a good example of that.

If you're a fan of war fiction, if you've read *The Sergeant,* or even Levinson's other series *The Rat Bastards* (about the war in the Pacific, originally published under the pseudonym John Mackie), you'll definitely want to check out *Doom Platoon.*

James Reasoner writes on his online blog, *Rough Edges* (where many of these reviews originally appeared).

CONTRIBUTORS

Teel James Glenn, Author, Stuntman, actor and fight choreographer has created Fantasy, Sword & Sorcery Mysteries, and contributed to anthologies

Teel James Glenn

including Bold Venture Press' *Zorro: Swordplay and Romance*.

David Goudsward

David Goudsward is the author of numerous articles on genealogy and New England megalithic sites as well as the books *America's Stonehenge: The Mystery Hill Story* (2003), *Ancient Stone Structures of New England* (2006), *H. P. Lovecraft in the Merrimack Valley* (2013), *Horror Guide to Massachusetts* (2014), *Horror Guide to Florida* (2015), and *Horror Guide to Northern New England* (2017). Recent books include *The Westford Knight and*

Henry Sinclair (2020) and *Sun, Sand, and Sea Monsters* (2020). Current projects include volumes 4 & 5 in the *Horror Guide* series (southern New England and Pennsylvania) and a study of HP Lovecraft's visits to Florida.

Michah Swanson Harris covered King Kong in "The Rankin-Bass Kong" in *Wonder* magazine, and in a loose trilogy, *The Eldritch New Adventures of Becky Sharp* (Minor Profit

Micah Swanson Harris

Press), *Ravenwood, the Stepson of Mystery: Return of the Dugpa*, and *Jim Anthony: the Hunters* (with Joshua Reynolds) from Airship27 Publications.

Riley Hogan grew up in Texas and Alaska. He is the author of the historical fantasy novel *As Tartary Burns*. He has

Riley Hogan

written for the *Tales of the Shadowmen* anthology. He works as a locksmith. Rumors of a monster-hunting career remain unconfirmed.

Will Murray

William Patrick Murray is known for writing, under his own and pen names. A partial list of his work includes such pulp fiction characters as Doc Savage, Tarzan, King Kong, The Shadow, and The Destroyer. He has contributed to prose anthologies and written short stories of Superman, Batman, Wonder Woman, Spider-Man, Ant-Man, The Avenger, Green Hornet and The Hulk. His stories have included Zorro, the Phantom and Sherlock Holmes. He's created tales for Marvel Comics including Captain America, Thor, and Iron Man. Among his numerous credits is the 1979 Lamont Award for his contributions to the furtherance of pulp fiction research, 1999 Comic Book Marketplace award, 2011 Pulp Ark Award for Best Series Revival for his work on *The Wild Adventures of Doc Savage*. His Doc Savage novel, *Doc Savage: Skull Island*, won the 2014 Pulp Factory Award for Best Novel. In 2021, the Golden Lion Award for his contributions of Tarzan created by Edgar Rice Burroughs. He received the First Fandom Hall of Fame Award in 2023 for his many career achievements.

Dr. Richard A. Olson

Dr. Richard A. Olson is also known as 'Dr. Batman,' a nickname arising from his love of the famous comic book character. A former rock drummer, martial artist, and bodybuilder, his is currently a Doctor of Chiropractic and Acupuncturist. He is the author of *A Man of Stihl: Nick Stihl, Private Investigator* and *Scott Lund, The Border Agent*. Recently, a collection of Nick Stihl stories, *Peoria Nights*, was released from Bold Venture Press.

Bart Pierce

Bart Pierce, an unrepentant monster kid, inspired by the stopmotion epics of O'Brien (*King Kong*) Ray Harryhausen the *Sinbad* sagas), began his professional film career as innovator of the in-your-face gore effects for Sam Raimi's horror classic, *Evil Dead*. After 15 years at 20th Century Fox creating Special Editions of classic films, like *Alien* and *Aliens*, he currently enjoys working with his spawn, Brett and Drew Pierce, (*The Sons of the Evil Dead*) on their successful, horror film careers, (*The Wretched* and *Deadheads*) while promoting a "Making of King Kong" screenplay.